CUPHEAD

in CARNIVAL CHAOS

by Ron Bates
With Illustrations by Studio MDHR's Lance Miller

Little, Brown and Company
New York Boston

This book is a work of fiction. Names, characters, places, and incidents are the product of the author's imagination or are used fictitiously. Any resemblance to actual events, locales, or persons, living or dead, is coincidental.

Art & Story Direction by Studio MDHR.
Illustrations by Studio MDHR's Lance Miller.

Cover design by Ching N. Chan & Studio MDHR. Cover illustration by Studio MDHR's Lance Miller.

Little, Brown and Company
Hachette Book Group
1290 Avenue of the Americas, New York, NY 10104
Visit us at LBYR.com
cupheadgame.com

First Edition: March 2020

Little, Brown and Company is a division of Hachette Book Group, Inc. The Little, Brown name and logo are trademarks of Hachette Book Group, Inc.

Library of Congress Cataloging-in-Publication Data
Names: Bates, Ron, author. | Miller, Lance, illustrator.
Title: Cuphead in Carnival chaos / by Ron Bates; with illustrations by Studio MDHR's Lance Miller.
Other titles: Carnival chaos
Description: First edition. | New York: Little, Brown and Company, 2020. | Audience: Ages 8-12. | Summary: "Cuphead and Mugman need to find the perfect gift for Elder Kettle's birthday, but with the carnival in town, can they escape the chaos and get their gift before it's too late?"—Provided by publisher.
Identifiers: LCCN 2019048852 | ISBN 9780316456548 | ISBN 9780316456517 (ebook) | ISBN 9780316456555 (ebook other)
Classification: LCC PZ7.B3778 Cup 2020 | DDC [Fic]—dc23
LC record available at https://lccn.loc.gov/2019048852

ISBNs: 978-0-316-45654-8 (paper over board), 978-0-316-45651-7 (ebook)

Printed in the United States of America

LSC-H

10 9 8 7 6 5 4 3 2 1

For Walt, who made it cool to wear big, fuzzy ears as a hat.

—Ron Bates

For Doutzen, Hans, and Hugo. May your lives be filled with wondrous stories.

—Chad & Maja Moldenhauer

1

THE DAWN PATROL

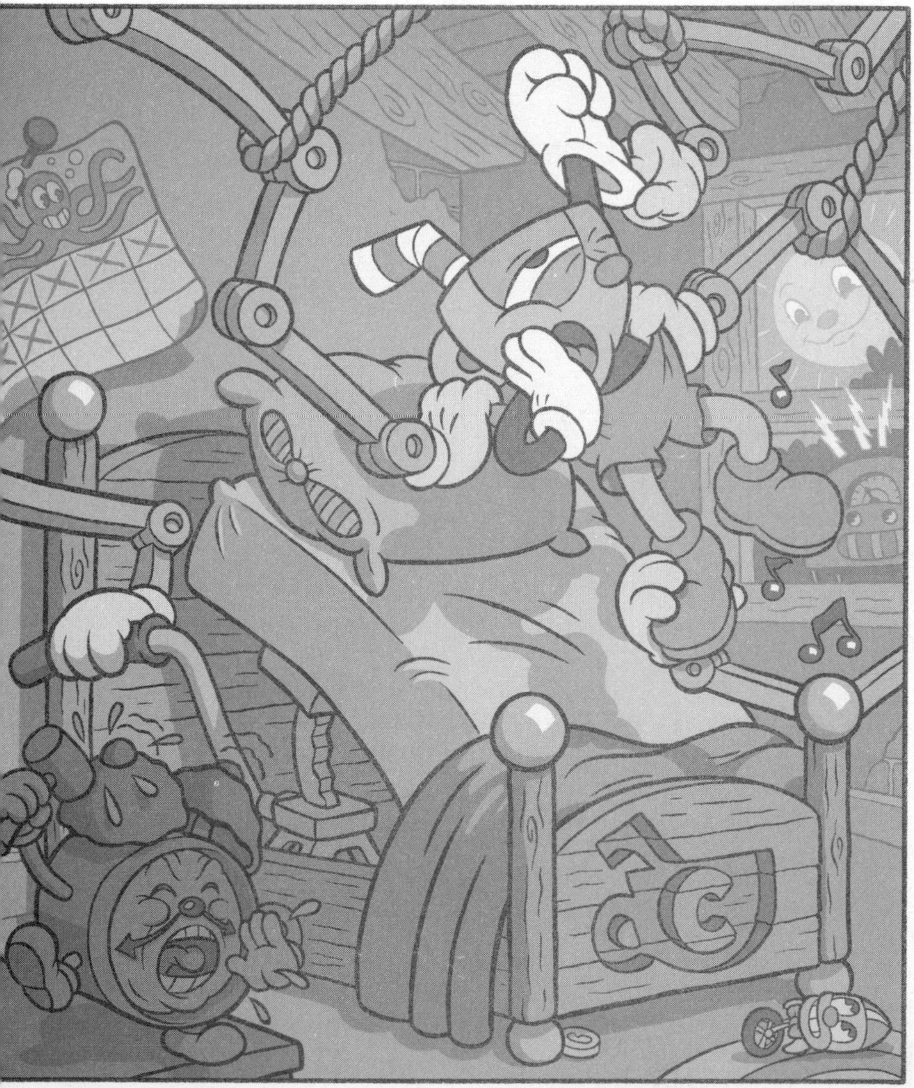

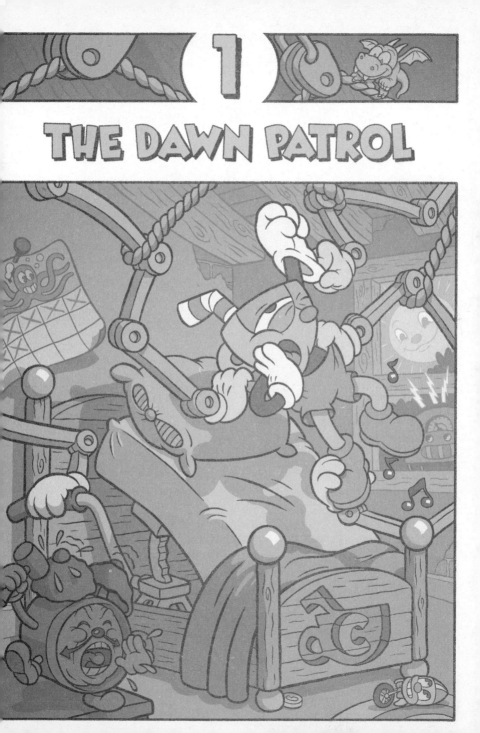

*C*LANG! CLANG! CLANG! CLANG! CLANG!

"It's morning, it's morning, it's morning!" the alarm clock screeched. "Up and at 'em! Let's get movin'! Rise and *shiiiiiiiiine!*"

The alarm clock sounded even more alarmed than usual, and who could blame him? It was past seven o'clock—eleven seconds past, to be exact. That meant there were only 61,189 seconds left in the entire day! And on a day as special as this, every single one of them was too precious to waste.

"Wake up, wake up, *WAKE UP!*" he bellowed.

His voice rumbled across the room, and down the stairs, and out over the Inkwell Isles, where it made quite an impression on the neighbors. The Potato family's eyes popped open, the Cornstalks covered their ears, and the Cow sisters (who always seemed to have the jitters, poor things) gave milkshakes that day.

But Cuphead? He kept right on snoozing.

This surprised no one, of course—Cuphead was Cuphead. He preferred to wake up in his own way, thank you very much, and no amount of clanging or banging or pushing or prodding would change that.

The alarm clock sighed. This being a special day and all, he'd hoped they wouldn't have to go through the whole routine, but...oh well, there was no use putting it off. He gripped the shiny brass bell above his head and pulled it down until it fit him like an army helmet. Then he marched to the edge of the night table, raised his minute hand, and with the steely gaze of a general, waved the signal flag.

Operation Beddy-Bye-Bye had begun.

As usual, the radio was the first to see the signal. He was tuned in to everything happening around here, not that he ever got any credit for it. But he'd show them—he'd show them all. This was his chance to prove he was more than just the golden-voiced broadcaster of shows like *Heebie Jeebie Theatre* and *Wyatt Burp: Rootin' Tootin' Root Beer Mug*. He could be inspiring, too. And this was his moment. He took a deep breath, twisted the oversize knob on his brown wooden chassis, and blasted out a barrage of earsplitting, heart-pounding, troop-rallying marching tunes. (Personally, he felt "Battlefield Boogie" and "Jeepers the Jivin' Jeep" would be best for marching. After all, they worked for the Lindy Hop.)

Now it was the dresser's turn. She opened her top drawer and the Clean Berets—a gutsy battalion of fancy French headwear—burst out. They leaped from the drawer, pulled their rip cords, and floated to the ground under a canopy of white linen handkerchiefs. There they joined the socks (who were foot soldiers), the suspenders (who were support units), the spectacles (who were lookouts), and the gloves (who were just plain handy), and together, they did what had to be done. First, they rolled out a big ball of twine and tugged on it until they'd run a long, long string around the room . . . *all* around the room. They ran it around the doorknob, the knickknacks, the lampshade, the curtain rod, a pair of bookends, and a polka-dot umbrella. When they finished, Sergeant Boxer (a plucky pair of green skivvies from the underwear drawer) tied the end of the string to Cuphead's bedpost.

The other end, they tied to an electric fan.

"Now!" the alarm clock called to the socks.

The Argyle twins—Lefty and Roger—plugged in the fan. As the blades spun faster and faster and faster, the string coiled around them like spaghetti on a fork. Then everything started to move. The doorknob turned, the knickknacks knocked, the lampshade crumpled, the curtain rod rattled, the bookends bumped, the umbrella opened, and finally Cuphead's bed, which had until that very moment been reliably horizontal, suddenly stood straight up like a buck private on inspection day. It bolted upright with such speed and fury that Cuphead was catapulted out from under his covers, into the air, and across the room.

But oddly enough, he did not crash. Or bash. Or splat. He didn't do any of those things. Instead, he landed—quite comfortably—in the pants, shirt, and shoes he'd laid out the night before.

"*Ahhhhhhh!* Good morning, everybody!" He yawned.

The whole room cheered.

Cuphead liked mornings. They were the start of a brand-new day—a day when anything could happen! He smiled, saluted his friend the alarm clock, and strutted across the room to a large wall calendar with a picture of an octopus on it.

"Yup, this is it," he said, drawing a big red circle around the date.

Well, as everyone knows, a big red circle on a calendar means only one thing: This is a special day. And he was about to write something inside that circle that would've explained just how special this day really was, but he couldn't.

The octopus had taken his pencil.

"Hey! What's the big idea?" Cuphead roared.

The octopus winked. A squishy green tentacle popped out of the picture and drew a big red X next to Cuphead's big red circle. Cuphead snatched the pencil and drew a second circle next to the big red X. The octopus drew another X, Cuphead drew another circle, and so it went until one of them had three in a row, making him the international tic-tac-toe champion of Cuphead's bedroom. There was a brief award ceremony followed by the shaking of hands and hands and more hands, because congratulations take a while when one of the players has eight arms.

But finally they were done and Cuphead could

return to his original task—writing *Elder Kettle's birthday!* in the first red circle on the calendar. Yes sirree, it was a very special day.

Then, as the radio blared out a jumpin', jivin' number by Flimm Flamm and His Tubadors (the swingin'est band in dancin' land), Cuphead bebopped out of the room and headed down to breakfast.

2

FAKIN' AND EGGS

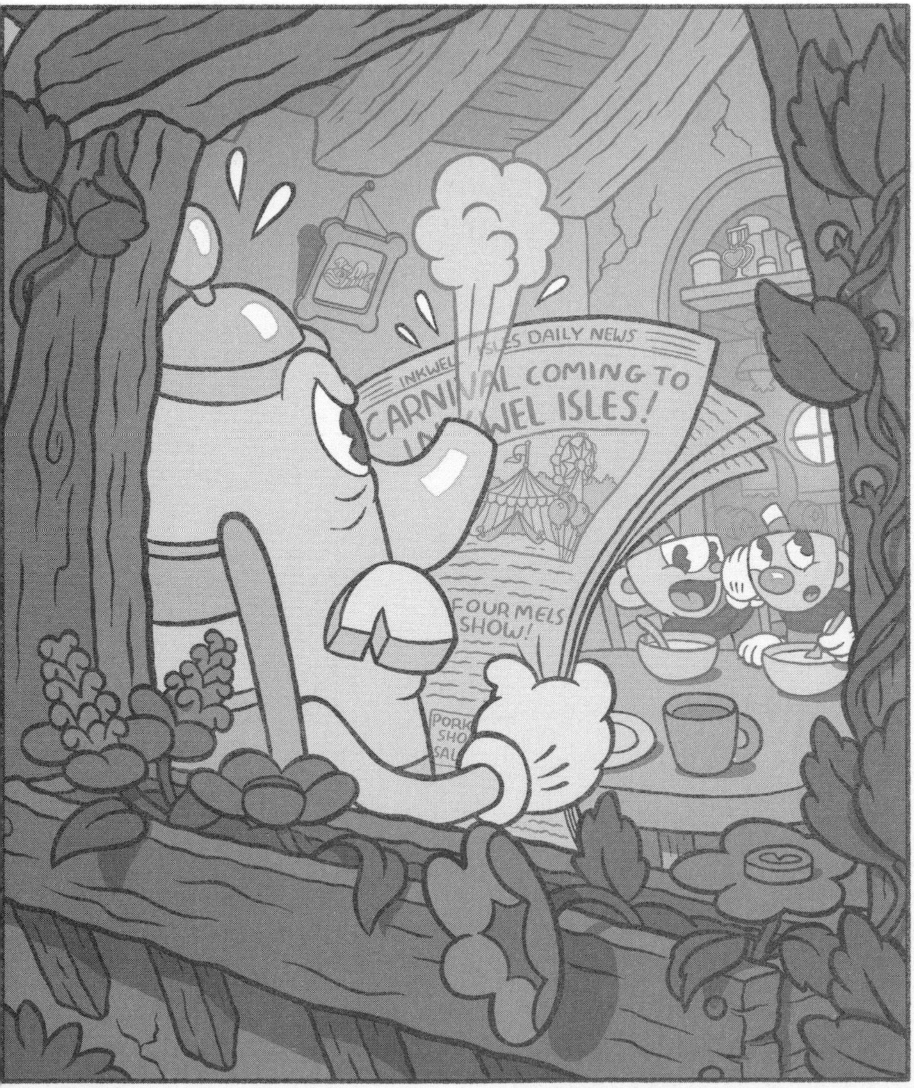
INKWEL
ISLES DAILY NEWS
COMING TO
WEL ISLES!
FOUR MELS
SHOW!

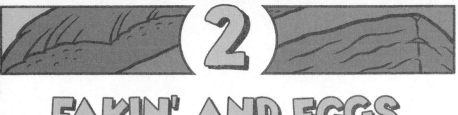

Cuphead and his younger brother, Mugman, lived with Elder Kettle in a neat little cottage on the edge of the Inkwell Isles. They were happy here, and Cuphead couldn't think of anywhere he'd rather live, or anyone he'd rather have as a guardian. After all, Elder Kettle was one of the kindest people on all the isles, and nearly everyone considered him a friend.

If anyone deserved a big birthday celebration, it was Elder Kettle. Cuphead could hardly wait for this evening to get here.

"Good morning, Cuphead," the old kettle chortled. "It's a lovely day, isn't it?"

"It's a humdinger," Cuphead told him.

But he didn't tell him anything else.

Elder Kettle made a little scowl. On this of all days, he'd expected a slightly different greeting from the young cup. He gave a lackluster flip to a flapjack in his skillet. (Elder Kettle was famous for his flapjacks, but this morning his heart wasn't in it.)

"Yes, a humdinger of a day," the kettle tried again. "I suppose you might even call it...special?"

He peeked at Cuphead out of the corner of his eye, but again, Cuphead didn't say a word. He just poured himself a big bowl of Mush Flakes and sat down at the table next to Mugman.

Elder Kettle paced back and forth, stroking his thick gray mustache. He wrinkled up his forehead until his eyebrows clanked together like a pair of colliding spoons.

"Gollywompers, it seems like there's something important about today, but for the life of me, I can't remember what it is," he said loudly. "Either of you boys know what it might be?"

Poor Elder Kettle. He wasn't just dropping hints; he was tying anchors to them. It was agony. So Cuphead (who was nothing if not compassionate) looked up from his bowl, stared into Elder's desperate, pleading eyes, and said—

"Nope."

Then he shoved the spoon back into his mouth.

"Oh, I know!" Mugman said excitedly. "It's your—"

WHACK!

Cuphead kicked his brother under the table. It wasn't a hard kick; it was the kind of kick you give to someone who's about to spill a very big secret about a very big surprise and make a large number of people *very* unhappy.

Mugman rubbed his leg.

"It's your, uh, imagination," he finished. "It must be. Because as far as I know, this is just another day."

He'd gotten Cuphead's message but still moved to the other side of the table. With a secret this big, you could never tell when another kick might be coming your way.

Elder Kettle let out a long, sad sigh. He was always excited about his birthday, and he'd been waiting all morning for someone to wish him well. But his friends hadn't called, the neighbors hadn't stopped by, and now even the boys had forgotten. The corners of his mouth sagged into a frown as he grumpily slid a half-burned flapjack onto Cuphead's plate. Oh well. Maybe it *was* just another day.

Knock, knock, knock!

Or maybe it wasn't! Someone was here! Someone had remembered! Elder Kettle rushed to the door wondering which wonderful, considerate, thoughtful neighbor had come to see him. As it turned out, it was none of them.

It was Hilda Berg.

Hilda Berg wasn't a wonderful, considerate, thoughtful neighbor. Hilda Berg was a pest. Elder Kettle tried to hide his disappointment, but it wasn't easy. Hilda was a tough one to like. First of all, she thought she was just a little bit above everyone else on the isles. True, she was a zeppelin and she *did* live in the sky, but did she have to be so snooty about it? Also, she was perpetually angry. Elder Kettle didn't know why she'd come to see him this morning, but he was sure it wasn't to say happy birthday.

"Good morning, Hilda," he said.

"Good?" Hilda sneered. "You think this is a *good* morning?"

Oh, what a shock—Her Dirigibleness wasn't happy. Elder Kettle sighed.

"What's the problem?"

Hilda glared at him, her nostrils flared, and her body inflated to a size so large he thought she was going to explode.

"The problem," barked Hilda, "is this!"

She lifted a tightly clenched fist (which was a scary sight on the best of days), and in it was a ball. It was round and white with horseshoe-shaped stitching along the edges, and it looked just like every other ball except for one thing. On the back side, scribbled in large black letters, were these words: PROPERTY OF CUPHEAD.

"Yesterday, I was tending my cloud garden—the loveliest in the entire sky, mind you—when this hideous projectile came crashing through it. It completely destroyed my prizewinning airigolds!" she snapped.

Airigolds, for anyone who's never seen them, are charming little puffballs made of only the most heavenly cloud material. Each flower rests on a slender cloud stem with wispy white leaves that flutter gently in the wind—unless, of course, they're smashed by a home run.

Elder Kettle scratched his chin.

"I see," he said. "Well, I'm very sorry, Hilda. But I'm sure it was an accident."

"An accident? It was a tragedy!" she cried. "Do you have any idea how difficult it is to raise a cloud garden? Each bloom must be coaxed from the delicate mist, then lovingly shaped into a precious form. I've spent weeks perfecting my airigolds. Then, in one thoughtless instant, that cloud wrecker—"

Her bony, accusing finger pointed straight at Cuphead, who was still at the table. He gave her an apologetic look. And he would've gladly explained to her that he'd made the hit of his life yesterday, the kind that climbs higher and higher and you think it's never going to come down (but you're still surprised when it doesn't), and he certainly hadn't been aiming at her cloud. But of course, he couldn't tell her that—or anything else—because he had half a flapjack stuffed into his cheeks and it was impolite to talk with his mouth full.

Elder Kettle shook his head.

"I'll speak with Cuphead, Hilda," he said.

"See that you do," she told him. "That boy is a menace. If he crosses me again, I'll deal with him myself!"

Elder Kettle bit his lower lip and a little puff of steam rose out of his spout. He didn't like threats, not first thing in the morning and definitely not on his birthday. He thought about slamming the door but, of course, he didn't. Elder Kettle could never be rude to anyone. Not even to Hilda Berg.

"Good day, Hilda," he said.

"Good day, indeed!" she grumbled, and stormed away down the path.

Elder Kettle closed the door and walked back to the breakfast table. He raised a disapproving eyebrow at Cuphead, but then set the ball by his breakfast plate.

"That must've been quite a hit. I wish I'd seen it," he said, and smiled.

Cuphead smiled back. He was glad Elder Kettle wasn't angry, and even gladder to have his ball back. There was nothing in the world Cuphead loved more than playing ball.

Elder Kettle sat down in his chair and drummed his fingers on the table. He really shouldn't let Hilda upset him—not on his birthday. He leaned back, picked up the newspaper, and opened it.

"Hey! I know what special thing is happening today," Mugman said, and Cuphead's eyes grew to the size of donuts. "The carnival is coming!"

"Carnival?" Elder Kettle yelled.

Mugman nodded. "It's right there in the news-paper."

Sure enough, on the front page was a big, bold

headline that read CARNIVAL COMING TO THE INKWELL ISLES.

Elder Kettle frowned.

"Oh no, not the carnival. Not here," he groaned. "Not again."

His mind drifted back to a time when he was a very young kettle. It was the last time the carnival had come to the Inkwell Isles. He remembered every sight and sound and scent. But mostly he remembered the clown who had approached him the instant he'd walked through the gate.

Guess your weight, sonny? the clown had asked in a chillingly spooky voice.

Okay, the little kettle had replied.

The clown had then lifted him into the air and shook him up and down and side to side, and never did guess his weight. But in the process, every coin had fallen out of the kettle's pockets and he'd left the carnival without a cent.

Elder Kettle told the boys the frightening story. They needed to know.

"I want you to stay away from that carnival," he said. "It's filled with liars and thieves."

The boys promised.

"It's time for school; go get your things," Elder Kettle said.

As Cuphead climbed back up the stairs, he thought about the carnival. He'd heard of carnivals, of course, but he'd never been to one—what were they like? Were they really as bad as Elder Kettle said? And if they were, why did people go to them? Not that it mattered, since he and Mugman had promised they'd stay away. Besides, if this carnival were any fun at all, the kids at school would be talking about it, and he hadn't heard a word. So it wasn't like he would really be missing out on anything—would he? No, he wouldn't be—carnivals were bad places and that's all there was to it. Anyway, tonight he had bigger plans. *Much* bigger plans.

This was going to be the best birthday of Elder Kettle's life!

3

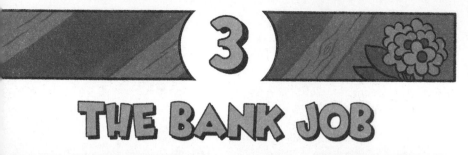

THE BANK JOB

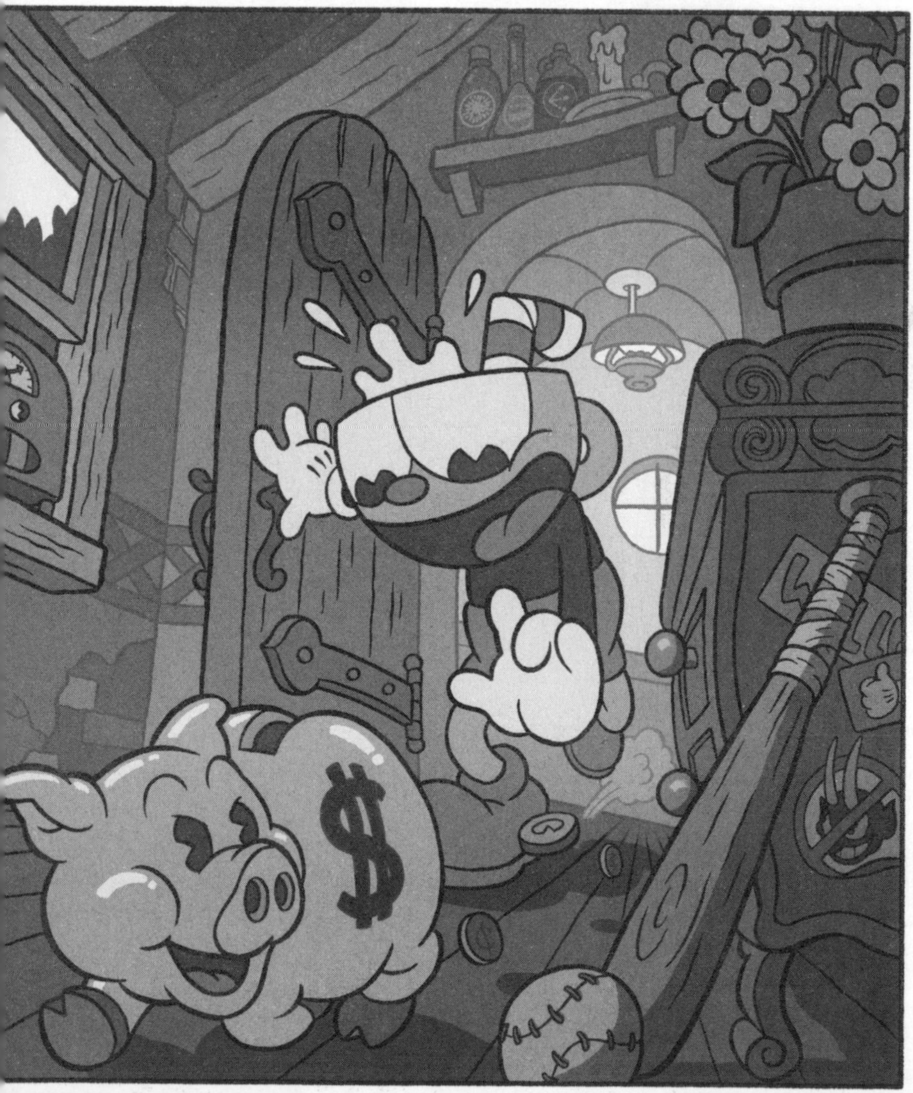

Cuphead walked into his bedroom. It looked different now, not at all like the wild wake-up scene from earlier. Everything was back in its place. Well, almost everything. He took the ball Hilda Berg had been nice enough to return (maybe she wasn't so bad after all) and put it on the high shelf near the bookcase. And as long as he was in the neighborhood—

"*SQUEEEEEEAAAAAAL!*"

He grabbed Piggy.

"Hey, hey, watch it there!" the pink ceramic piggy bank squealed. "Take it easy, will you?"

"Sorry, Piggy," Cuphead said, shaking him a little so he could hear the coins jingle.

"Well, I'm not a piñata, you know—so don't get any ideas," the pig said. "What are you doing, anyway?"

Cuphead looked around the room to make sure no one was listening. He lowered his voice to a whisper.

"I'm getting everything ready for"—he looked around again—"Elder Kettle's birthday party."

"Birthday party!" Piggy yelled.

"*Shhhhhh!* Will you be quiet? He's going to hear you."

"So let him hear me. I love birthday parties! When's the happy occasion?"

"Tonight, and you're invited. But it's a surprise," Cuphead said.

He turned the pig upside down and shook him again.

"Hey, stop that! You're making me dizzy!"

"Well, I'm sorry, but I need to get the money out for the present."

"Money?" Piggy gasped.

He leaped out of Cuphead's hands and landed on the bed. Suddenly, it all made sense. For the past few weeks, Cuphead had been stuffing him with money—fistfuls of it. It was a piggy bank's dream! He was actually full for the first time in his life. And now Cuphead thought he could just come and take it back?

"Never!" Piggy cried.

Cuphead rolled his eyes. He'd been afraid this would happen. The gobs of money he and Mugman had been collecting came from Elder Kettle's friends so they could all go in together on a really nice present, the kind that would make this birthday unforgettable. But Piggy wasn't used to seeing so such money. And now that he'd developed a taste for it...

This wasn't going to be easy.

"Calm down, Piggy. Let's talk this over," Cuphead said.

"There's nothing to talk about. That money is the official property of the First National Bank of Piggy—which is me! So back off!"

This was ridiculous. Cuphead was going to be late for school. He leaped onto the bed and made an attempt at a tackle, but Piggy squirmed out of his grasp.

"Help! Police! Bank robbery!" the pig squealed.

Piggy jumped off the bed, and Cuphead went after him. As they raced around the room, others joined the chase. The dresser moved in from the right side, while the radio blocked the left side, and the alarm clock tried to ambush him from above. But the pig was too quick for all of them. Finally, they managed to corner him near the window.

"Stay away, stay away!" he warned them.

"Aw, jeepers, Piggy, be a sport," Cuphead said. "I'm going to be late for school!"

But Piggy crossed his arms and shook his head defiantly.

"I'm never giving you this money—not one red cent. And there's nothin' you can do about it!"

Cuphead frowned. Piggy was greedy and amazingly stubborn. This could take all day. But maybe there was another way.

"Okay, I believe you, you're never going to give me the money. But what if I trade you something for it?" he asked.

"Trade?" Piggy said. "Trade what?"

Cuphead pulled a yellow flower out of a pot on the windowsill. Piggy's eyes widened.

"Is that a—a—a—?"

"Is it a what?" Cuphead asked innocently.

He held the flower out and wiggled it against Piggy's nose.

"Get that thing away from me!"

"Why? Does it bother you?"

He wiggled it again.

"No fair!" Piggy groaned. "You know that I'm allergic to rhodo . . . rho-do . . . rho-do-do—"

He scrunched up his face and put a finger

under his snout. "RHO-DO-DENDRONS! AH-CHOOOOOOOOOOOO!"

The sneeze shook the room like a thousand Ala-ka-BLAM firecrackers bursting at once. When it was over, money floated down from above like freshly minted snowflakes. Cuphead quickly scooped it all up and stuffed it in his pocket.

"Thanks, Piggy," he said. "See you at the party!"

Then he grabbed his books, slid down the staircase banister, and ran out the front door with Mugman.

"Remember what I told you," Elder Kettle called after them. "Stay away from that carnival!"

4
CUPHEAD PLANS A PARTY

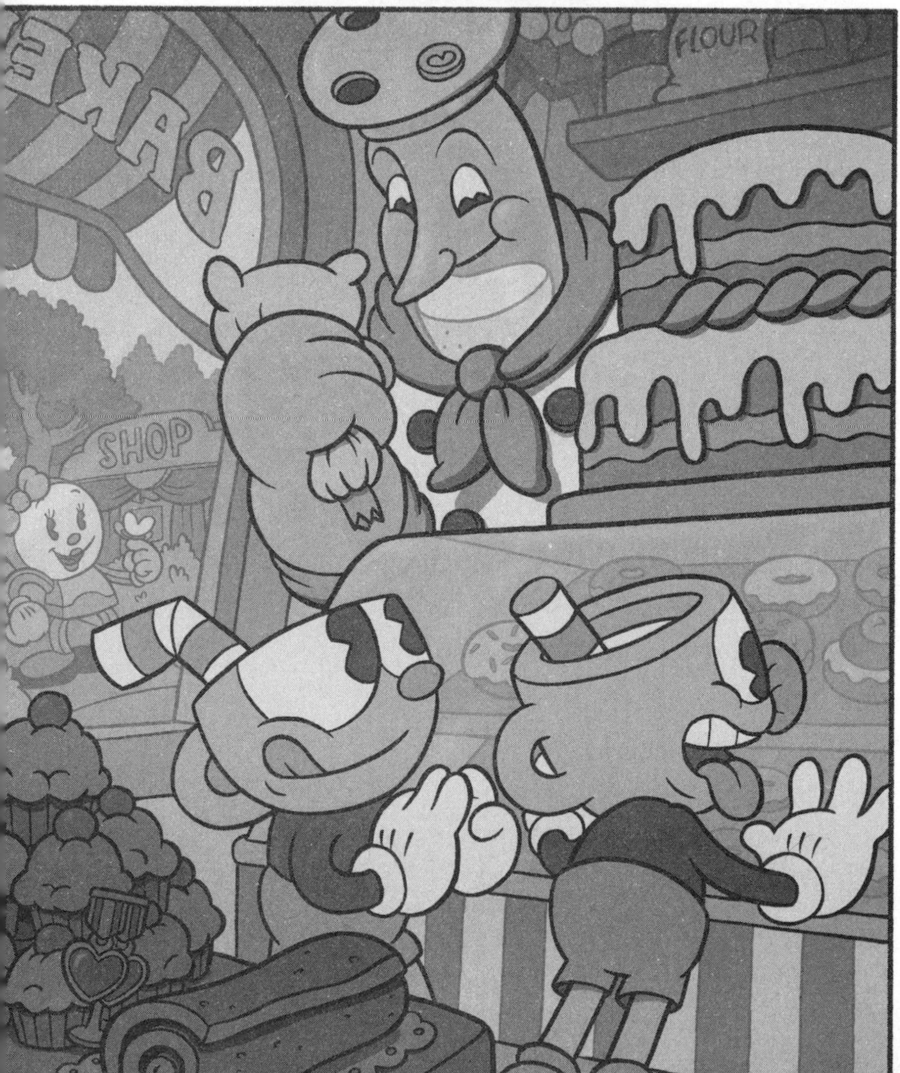
BAKE
FLOUR
SHOP

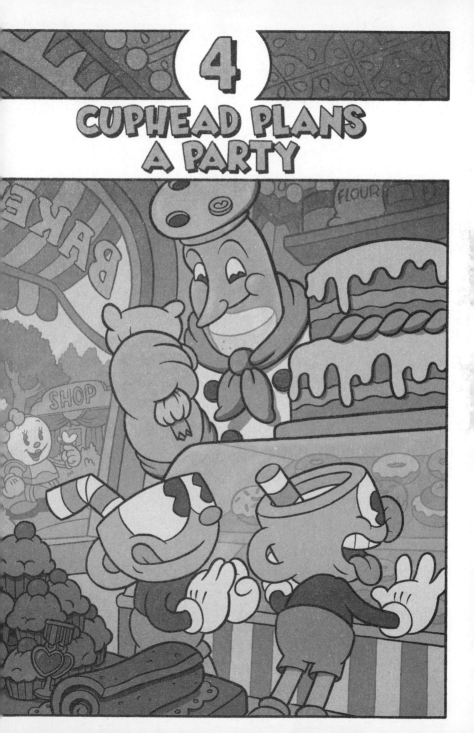

On the way to school, Cuphead and Mugman saw the same familiar faces they always saw on their walk. They waved to Mr. Milky, who drove the milk wagon; said good morning to Mrs. Frosty, who drove the ice wagon; and gave a quick hello to Ollie Bulb, the grocer.

"Hello, Cuphead! Hello, Mugman!" cried Ollie.

And then he cried some more. He wept with joy at the sight of them, because, well, Ollie wept about everything. It's probably because he's an onion, and, as you know, they're very sensitive vegetables. So the tears poured like summer rain, but no one minded, including Ollie, because there's nothing he enjoyed more than a good cry.

"Are you coming to the you-know-what tonight?" Cuphead asked.

"You mean the party? Wouldn't miss it!" cried Ollie.

"*Shhhhh!* Remember, it's a surprise!"

"A surprise? Me and my big mouth!" Ollie replied, and the tears poured out again.

The hardest thing about having a surprise birthday party is making sure it stays a surprise. That was especially true on the Inkwell Isles. It was such a tiny community. Everyone knew one another, and there were gossips everywhere. Those people couldn't wait to blab the latest news, and Elder Kettle's birthday was *very* big news. It was going to be a huge celebration! There'd be music and dancing and, of course, a cake. Not just any cake, mind you—for an occasion like this, Chef Saltbaker was whipping up something extra special.

Chef Saltbaker was a tall, distinguished-looking saltshaker with a friendly smile and a shiny topper. His bakery was a very busy place. When Cuphead and Mugman stopped by, the chef was hard at work while spatulas, eggbeaters, spoons, and the other utensils rushed about in a culinary frenzy.

"Hello, Chef," Cuphead said warmly. "Is the cake ready yet?"

Suddenly, everything in the busy kitchen stopped and the whole place fell silent.

"Ready?" Chef Saltbaker asked, sounding a little

offended. "You want to know if the cake I'm making is ready?"

He turned to his kitchen utensils.

"Did you hear that? He wants to know if the cake is ready! Ha!"

"Ha–ha–ha–ha–ha!" the utensils all laughed.

"Oh look, zee cake, she is ready. We'll put it in a paper bag for you! Ha–ha–ha!" a spatula joked. "What does he think you're making? A cupcake?"

The utensils laughed again. Cuphead didn't know why, but apparently, he'd asked the funniest question they'd ever heard.

"The cake will be ready exactly when the time is right and not a minute before," the chef told him. "I will not serve a creation this delicious at anything other than the absolute peak of freshness."

Cuphead nodded, but he was shuffling his feet.

"Well, I just thought, since the party's tonight, you might want to have it done early."

Now the entire kitchen glared at him.

"Oh, make the cake early? What a wonderful idea! 'Here you are, Elder Kettle. Enjoy your stale, tasteless, day-old cake.' Pishposh!" Chef said, then added sheepishly, "Please excuse my salty language."

Chef was an artist and a genius and a very nice guy. But he was passionate about baking. Cuphead should've known better than to question his work.

"Well, maybe the cake isn't ready, but something sure smells good," Mugman said.

Now Chef smiled.

"In my shop, everything smells good. Because everything is good! Here, lick these spoons!"

They did.

"*Mmmmmmmmmmm*," Cuphead said. "What is it?"

"Perfection," said Chef. "Now run along, I have a masterpiece to create."

Cuphead and Mugman left the bakery which, as luck would have it, was currently right next door to Porkrind's store. They still needed to find a gift for Elder Kettle.

They opened the door and went inside.

"What do you want?" said Porkrind.

Porkrind was a rough-looking swine with an eye patch and a gruff, gravelly voice. He wasn't great with customers, but his store always had interesting things.

"We're looking for a present for Elder Kettle," Cuphead explained. "It's his birthday."

"Birthday, huh? How about socks?" Porkrind asked. "Everybody needs socks."

"No," said Cuphead. "Not socks."

"Suspenders?"

"No."

"Mustache wax? Shoelaces? Liniment oil?"

"It's for his birthday; it needs to be . . . classy. You know, something fancy."

Porkrind rolled his un-patched eye.

"Well, pardon me, Mr. Ooh-la-la," he grunted, then turned and picked up a glass bottle from a shelf. "How about some smelly French *co-log-nee*? Or ain't that good enough for His *Majesty*?"

Cuphead sighed. There were times when he wished Porkrind didn't have the only gift shop in town.

"What about this?" said Mugman.

He was standing in the corner of the store, staring at a shelf filled with toy airplanes. They had birchwood gliders and windup planes and even a gas-powered flyer. For as long as he could remember, Mugman had been fascinated by planes.

"Jeepers, Mugman, Elder Kettle doesn't want some dumb toy," Cuphead told him. "It's got to be something like—"

And then he saw it. Inside a case just beneath the cash register was the perfect thing. It was a pocket watch—a shiny, gold watch with a shimmering chain.

"That! That's exactly what we . . . oh my gosh, look what time it is!"

The big hand on the pocket watch was pointing to the eleven. That meant they had just five minutes before the tardy bell rang.

"Come on, Mugman," Cuphead said. "We'll come back after school."

They rushed out the door.

"We close at four o'clock on the dot," Porkrind called after them. "Don't be late!"

"We won't be!" Cuphead called back.

As they raced down the street toward the schoolhouse, they spotted a big crowd of people gathered in the town square. Cuphead couldn't see what they were looking at, only that they were excited. But he could see the top of a big, colorful tent being raised into the air. It was beautiful! He froze, staring at it.

"Come on, ya big dope," Mugman said, and he grabbed Cuphead by the collar and dragged him down the street.

5

A FORK IN THE ROAD

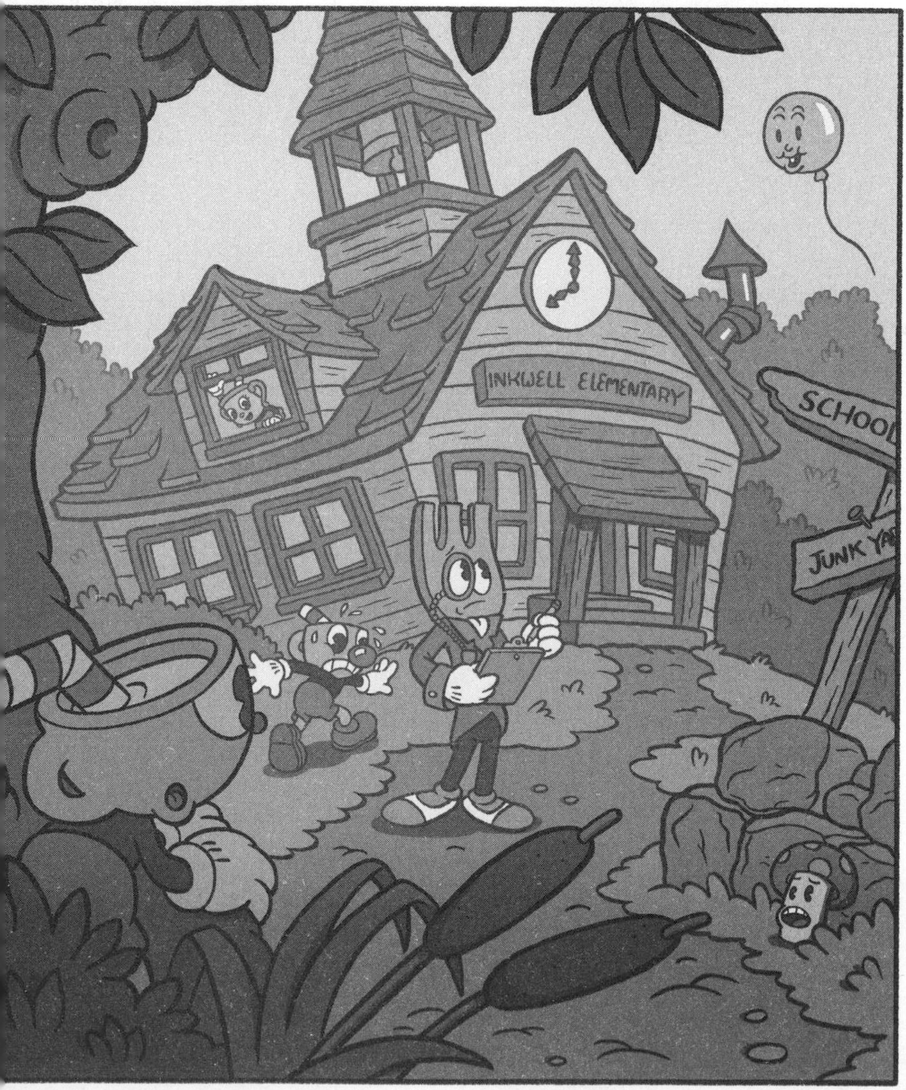
INKWELL ELEMENTARY
SCHOO
JUNK YA

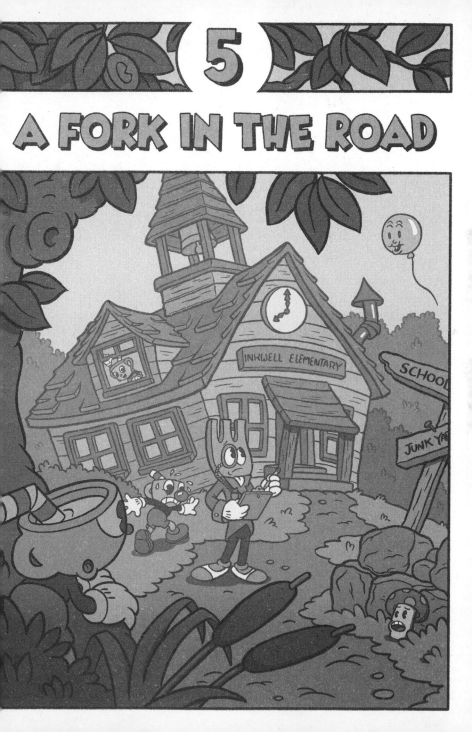

Ahuge, billowy cloud of dust rose behind the
brothers as they ran down the old school road.
It wasn't the usual kind of running, you understand;
it was the kind that spins mailboxes round like weather
vanes and pulls the feathers off nearby chickens.
Needless to say, this made a mess of the mail that day
and greatly embarrassed a group of hens who were out
for their morning stroll, but it couldn't be helped.
Cuphead and Mugman simply could not be late. Not
on this day. That would be a disaster.

Unfortunately, the only thing moving faster than
they were was the clock on the front of the large
schoolhouse. It was the most annoying clock on the
isles, never helpful when you needed it to be, never
lending you a few seconds that you could pay back
tomorrow or whenever you had some spare time. No,
this was one of those clocks that moved too quickly

in the morning, then took its dear sweet time getting through the rest of the day. The worst part was that the clock had it in for Cuphead. He was absolutely sure of it.

"Almost there!" called Cuphead, wheezing like a teakettle that's nearly out of steam.

He was trying to be encouraging (Cuphead could find the bright side of a situation even when there wasn't one), but as it happened, he was right. The school was just around the next corner. It was going to be close—down to the wire, really—but with the wind at their backs and a little luck, they might actually make it. Cuphead could picture it now: He and Mugman walking in with the other kids, getting their usual welcome from Mat, the welcome mat.

"Good morning, ow! Welcome to school, *ow!*" Mat would say as the crowd tramped on his face. "Nice to see you, have a terrific day, *owwwww!*"

Nothing perked up a morning like Mat's cheerful scream beneath your feet, and Cuphead was determined to hear it. He urged Mugman on. The two of them pumped their arms and gritted their teeth, and that's when they saw it.

SCREEEEEEEEEEEEECH!

There was a fork in the road. It wasn't just any fork—you don't bring two pairs of virtually flying feet to a screeching halt over just any fork—it was Silverworth. Or as he was known to every school-age boy and girl on the Inkwell Isles, Principal Silverworth.

"Gee whillikers, it's the principal! Hide! Hide!" Cuphead said.

The two of them ducked into the bushes. It was a reflex action, an overwhelming impulse that came over them the second they saw the highfalutin fork standing between them and the school. Everyone knew how Silverworth felt about being on time.

"Punctuality is the key to educationality," he said as he pushed a group of students through the wide front door. "You may quote me."

Whenever Silverworth had something profound to say, and that was more often than you'd think, he would hold a single finger in the air as if posing for a statue. The truth is, he would not have been at all surprised to one day find tributes to him carved in marble or bronze or Limburger cheese or some other material that might be suitable for a particular occasion. After all, he was, in his humble opinion, a monumental sort of figure. A small but distinguished-looking fork, he wore a monocle because it was stylish, and passed out detention slips like a newsie delivering the *Inkwell Gazette*.

No one was better at catching a Late Kate or Tardy Marty than Principal Silverworth. He could smell a straggler a mile away, and while he hadn't yet spotted Cuphead and Mugman, he knew someone was out there. And he would find them. It was only a matter of time.

"*Hmmmmm*...If I were a lollygagger, where would I be?" he muttered to himself.

As luck would have it, that was the very moment that Canteen Hughes—who wore extremely thick goggles—happened to walk by. Silverworth plucked the lenses from Canteen's face and held them up like binoculars. He scanned the schoolyard.

"Now, where are you hiding?" he said.

There was no answer, of course, only the sound of Canteen Hughes walking blindly into a nearby post. Silverworth paid no attention. He was focused entirely on the task in front of him, and that meant Cuphead and Mugman were in a predicament.

"Don't worry," Cuphead said hopefully. "We're not licked yet."

RINGGGGGGGGGGGGGGGGGGGG!

Then again, he may have spoken too soon. Nothing says you're licked more loudly than the merciless clang of the tardy bell. Cuphead stared up at the face on the big clock at the front of the building and saw her smile. It was as if she had been deliberately waiting for them to get this close, so their defeat would be that much more painful.

Now they were trapped outside—just them and Silverworth.

The principal raised a finger.

"Lateness is an impediment to greatness," he called out. "This is valuable learning time you should be spending in the classroom, and you've already wasted—"

He turned to look at the clock behind him. When he did, Cuphead and Mugman picked up the bush and, like some kind of giant, leafy caterpillar, tiptoed closer to the front of the building. They set the shrubbery down again just as Silverworth turned back around.

"One minute," he announced.

Mugman and Cuphead stared at each other. A full minute—gone. Class would be starting, and they were sure to be missed. They needed a plan, and they needed it fast. So Mugman pulled out his thinking cap (which looked like a brain but with lightning bolts on the side and a propeller on top) and put it on. But before he had time to do even the slightest bit of thinking, he heard a strange noise like steam escaping from a radiator.

"*Pssssssssssssssst.*"

"Did you say something?" he whispered.

"No, I thought you said something," said Cuphead. "I was hoping you had an idea."

"Not a one," Mugman told him.

He went back to his thinking.

"*Pssssssssssssssst.*"

There was that sound again. Cuphead looked around.

"What is that?"

"I don't know," said Mugman, checking his cap. "Maybe my brain is leaking?"

But the noise was not coming from either of Mugman's brains. It was, in fact, coming from a second-story window on the side of the school building. If the boys had only looked up, they would have seen a bright-eyed classmate waving her arms in a desperate attempt to get their attention. Her name was

Ms. Chalice and she was a clever and fun-loving girl with a mischievous streak that frequently got them into trouble. She was also the best friend they'd ever had.

From the window, she'd been watching her pals' clumsy attempt to make it into the school. It was sad, really. They needed her help. Ms. Chalice liked helping the boys—what she did not like was being ignored. So she reached out, grabbed the drainpipe that ran down the side of the building, and tilted it until it hovered just above their shrubby hiding place. Then she held it up to her mouth and very discreetly— or as discreetly as can be expected when you're using an enormous metal megaphone—she said:

"I SAID, *PSSSSSSSSSSSSSSSSSSSSSSSSST!*"

The sound blasted a big flurry of leaves from the bush and not surprisingly got the boys' attention. When they saw her smiling and waving, they couldn't have been more relieved. After all, if there was one thing Ms. Chalice was better at than getting into trouble, it was getting out of it.

They watched as she pulled a yo-yo from her pocket and flung it forward. It *rolllllllllllllllllled* out on the long string until it was right in front of their faces, and then it stopped. Written on the side of it was a message.

Dear Tardy Twosome, it said.

She yanked the string and the yo-yo rolled back to her. When it rolled out again, there was another message.

Looks like you're having some trouble.

In short order, it rolled in and out again six more times with six more messages that, when put together, said:

Come to the window...

And I'll help you...

Get inside.

Warmest regards,

Ms. Chalice

PS: Impressive yo-yoing, isn't it?

The boys thought this was an excellent plan, the only flaw being that it had absolutely no chance of working. How were they supposed to get to the window with Silverworth standing only a few feet away? It was impossible! But just when it looked like all hope was lost, a light bulb appeared above Cuphead.

"You have an idea!" Mugman said excitedly.

"I do?" said Cuphead.

He wondered what it could be.

Still, there was no use wasting a perfectly good

light bulb. He reached up and plucked it out of the air, and it was a lucky thing he did, too. Because no sooner had he put that brilliant bubble in his hand than he really did get an idea. He was surprised it hadn't come to him sooner.

Taking a quick peek out of the bush, he cocked back his arm and, with the deadeye aim of a big-league pitcher, tossed the bulb toward the school entrance. It sailed past Silverworth, hurried straight through the doorway, and—*CRASH!*

"*Ouch!* I mean, welcome!" cried Mat.

Silverworth, who knew a clue when he heard one, whirled around to investigate. When his back was turned, the shrubbery again sprouted legs and ran to the side of the building. Now that they were under the window, the boys could hear their teacher, Professor Lucien, a very bookish bulb, calling roll.

"Canteen Hughes?"

"Here."

"Mac?"

"Here."

"Chip?"

"Here."

Yikes. He was already halfway through the list,

which meant they had to act fast. Fortunately, Ms. Chalice was still at the window.

"Grab hold," she whispered.

She flung the yo-yo down and Cuphead and Mugman dutifully grabbed it. An instant later, they found themselves rolling up the side of the building. With a quick, hard yank on the string, Ms. Chalice pulled the brothers through the window and spun them across the room like a couple of jumbo-size tops. They bounced from wall to wall and desk to desk and aisle to aisle, then teetered and tottered and—just when it looked like things might come to a disastrous end—wobbled past their classmates and plunked down in their seats. And not a moment too soon.

"Cuphead?" Professor Lucien called.

"Here!" Cuphead wailed. Then his desk toppled over like a top-heavy icebox.

"Are you all right?" the professor asked.

"Oh, he's right as rain," groaned Mugman, who was hugging the top of his own desk like a seasick sailor on a life raft. "And he'll be even better once the school stops spinning."

Now, for most people, if they were paying any attention at all, the brothers' behavior that morning would've seemed a tad unusual. But this never occurred to Professor Lucien. In fact, he hadn't even noticed. Please don't think this was because he was a bad teacher—quite the opposite. Lucien was a very good and kind teacher. But he was also the smartest person on the Inkwell Isles and, as any smart person will tell you, this can be a terrible burden. Regrettably, when your mind is filled with formulas and theorems and equations, there simply isn't room for very much more. That's why highly intelligent people tend to miss things like jokes and dental appointments and students being yo-yoed through the classroom window.

It's just their way.

From his spot on the floor, Cuphead soon realized two things: Professor Lucien needed new shoes, and the class was extremely excited about something. An electric murmur was coursing through the room, and while he couldn't make out everything, one word came through loud and clear:

Carnival!

6

CUPHEAD WRITES AN ESSAY

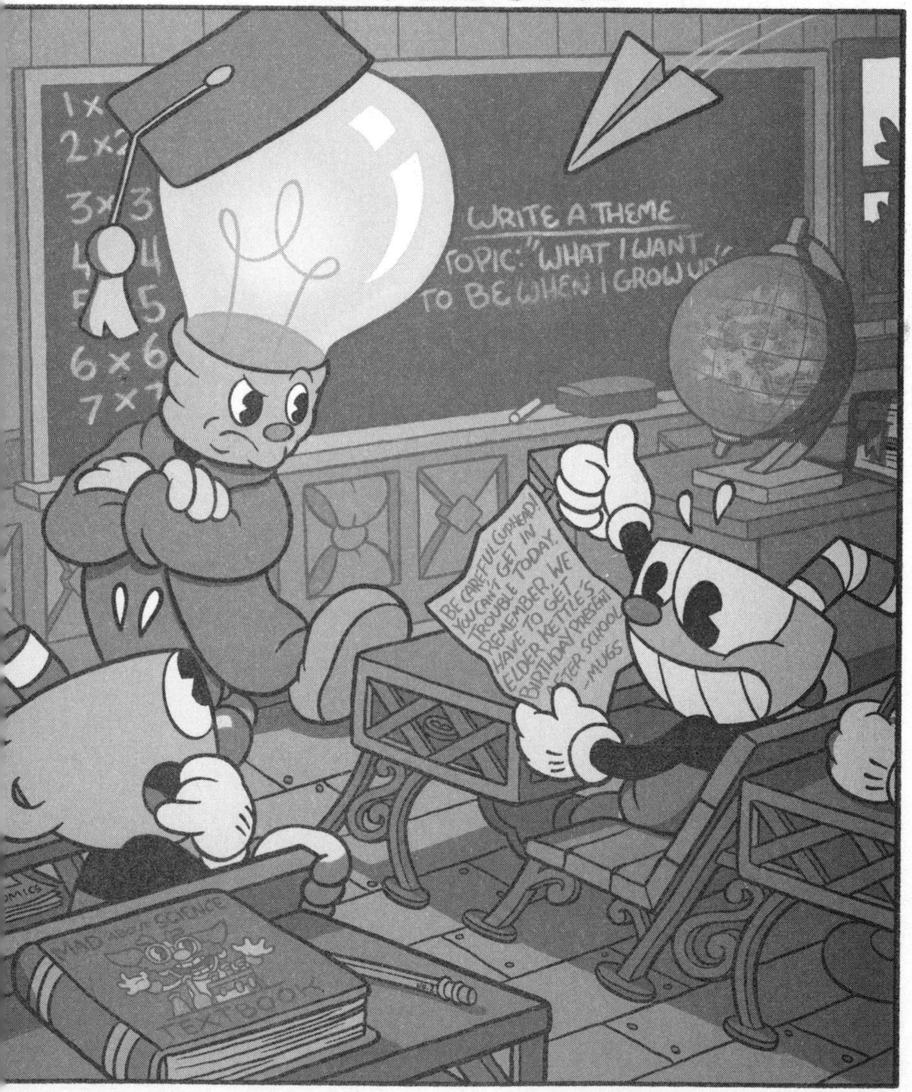
WRITE A THEME
TOPIC: "WHAT I WANT
TO BE WHEN I GROW U
BE CAREFUL CUPHEAD! YOU CAN'T GET IN TROUBLE TODAY. REMEMBER, WE HAVE TO GET ELDER KETTLE'S BIRTHDAY PRESENT AFTER SCHOOL. —MUGS
MAD ABOUT SCIENCE
TEXTBOOK

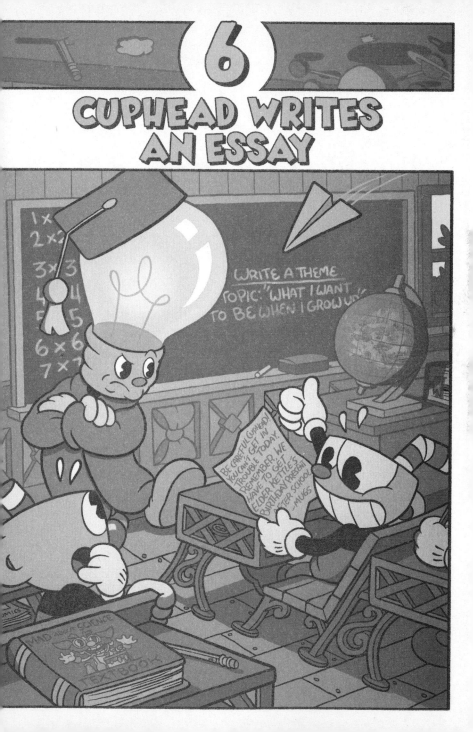

Are you going to the carnival, Cuphead?" Ginger asked him.

Ginger was a gingerbread girl who sat in the desk directly behind Cuphead's. Like most gingerbread girls, she was sweet. A little on the nosy side, maybe, but sweet.

"Well—" said Cuphead, climbing to his feet and setting his desk upright.

"Of course he's going. Everyone's going," Canteen Hughes interrupted. "What kind of lamebrain would miss the carnival? Did you see that roller coaster? It's a real doozy."

Roller coaster? There was a roller coaster? Cuphead gulped. He'd seen roller coasters in the newsreels at the movies. They looked like trains that got caught in a tornado and didn't know how to get out. Suddenly, he imagined his entire row of desks climbing up a tall track, and—*SWOOSH*—plunging down the other side. It was terrifying! The awful thought made his skin break out in goose bumps and, before he knew it, they were waddling down his arms and making embarrassing honking noises.

"Boy oh boy, a roller coaster," he said extra loudly. "I can hardly wait!"

It was the best he could come up with at the moment. The truth was, although Cuphead was very brave, the idea of getting on a roller coaster made him queasy. He wasn't scared, of course—not *really* scared—it was more of an allergy. Yes, that's it! He was allergic to being brutally mangled, and there was nothing anyone could do about it. So even though the carnival sounded like a swell place filled with all kinds of things that didn't twist or turn or flip upside down and give you an upset stomach, and he would give almost anything to see them, his hands were tied. If he were to set one foot in that world of wonders, the rest of the gang would expect him to join them on the dipping, diving death machine, and that was not going to happen.

Still, it was a shame to miss the whole carnival over one little roller coaster. It was like not eating an ice-cream sundae just because someone had put a snake in it. And who knew when he'd have this chance again? Maybe if he was extra careful and stayed *waaaaay* over on the other side of the grounds, then—

No, no, no, no, no. Elder Kettle had told him to keep away from it, and that's exactly what he was going to do. The birthday party would be thrilling enough, thank you very much.

"Quiet down, class," Professor Lucien said. "Your assignment this morning is to write an essay."

The class groaned. Lucien straightened his mortarboard and gave them a long, stern look.

"And the topic," he continued, "is 'What I want to be when I grow up.'"

Cuphead's eyes popped wide open. Usually essays were dull, boring, torturous projects about history or science or books. But this—this was about something important! At last, he could tell the world exactly what the future held for a boy named Cuphead. Then the praise would come rolling in!

He picked up his pencil. Rats! The tip was dull. This would never do—you couldn't write sharp literature with a dull pencil. With no time to spare, he quickly chewed the end like a wood chipper until it had a shiny new point. Now it was an instrument worthy of the task. He put it to paper.

What I Want to Be When I Grow Up. By Cuphead, he wrote. It sounded boffo already!

Ah, the future. He'd pictured it a thousand times. It was going to be glorious.

Cuphead leaned back in his desk and let the daydream take over. In his thoughts, he wasn't stuck in some boring ol' classroom. He was in a grand stadium, on the pitcher's mound with a horsehide ball in his hand. All around him, crowds were clapping and cheering as he tugged his cap, hiked up his knickers, and scorched batters like a pint-size flamethrower. Eventually, the fantasy became so big that it drifted out of his head in a puffy dream balloon and bumped up against the ceiling. And that's exactly where it would've stayed if it hadn't been for one thing.

Ms. Chalice.

You see, in the next desk over, Ms. Chalice was having a dream of her own, one that was every bit as big and bold and real as Cuphead's. This wasn't surprising—Ms. Chalice knew all about the dream world. Before she became the most interesting girl on the Inkwell Isles (which she undoubtedly was), she'd been a wise and benevolent spirit called the Legendary Chalice. The story of how she left the astral plane and became the witty, charming, happy-go-lucky best friend of Cuphead and Mugman is one about an incredible, amazing, fascinating quest—but that's a tale for another day.

Now, where were we? Ah yes, Ms. Chalice's dream. It was a thrilling adventure in which she was driving a racing car at top speed down a long, looping track. She could see herself in goggles and a helmet, gripping the wheel and zipping past rivals as she roared round and round the speedway. Before long, her dream, like Cuphead's, formed a puffy cloud that floated out of her head and up to the ceiling. The two dreams hovered side by side, and that's exactly where they would've stayed if it hadn't been for one other thing.

Mugman.

In the *next* desk over, Mugman's head was back and his eyes were closed, and he was soaring away on a pair of dreamy wings. You see, more than anything, Mugman wanted to be a flying ace. It was why he loved the planes he'd found in Porkrind's store. He could imagine himself high in the sky, having dogfights and doing loop de loops and aerial spins. And on this particular day, his imagination carried him so high that the dream cloud flew right out of the top of his head. When it reached the ceiling (which was unusually crowded that morning), it bumped against Ms. Chalice's racing dream, which bashed into Cuphead's ball-playing dream, and before you knew it, the three of them were floating toward the open window.

Here's the thing about having big dreams and a small window: It's a tight squeeze. So tight, in fact, that as the clouds tried to get through, they were squashed together into one giant super-cloud filled with ballparks and racetracks and runways and all the other things that had popped out of the young friends' minds. But after some scooching and squirming, the dreamy blob managed to make it outside. Once there, it climbed into the air and mixed in so well with all the other big, puffy clouds that no one could even tell the difference, and that was the end of that.

Or so it seemed.

If only Hilda Berg hadn't chosen that exact moment to fly past the school. But you know Hilda, always buzzing around the sky like she owns the place. As a zeppelin, she was at home in the clouds and cut through them as easily as strolling through the park.

Truth be known, she never gave it a thought—why would she? Clouds were filled with lots and lots of fluffy, misty nothingness, and not a single thing more.

Still, she did notice something odd about this cloud. For one thing, there was a big, grinning Mugman flying directly at her in what looked like a windup toy airplane. Stunned, she veered off course only to end up on a racetrack surrounded by speeding cars—which, as you know, are rare at that altitude. Before she could pull away, Ms. Chalice's dream racer blew past and whirled her into another part of the super-cloud, and at the worst possible time, too. Cuphead was just about to throw the final pitch in what was sure to be a no-hitter, when—

BONK.

He hit her.

Not on purpose, of course. Hilda just happened to fly directly into the path of Cuphead's blazing fastball. So instead of thudding against the leather of a catcher's mitt, it conked against the side of her head. Dazed and discombobulated, she lost control and flew straight for the stadium scoreboard, which—*SMACK!*—changed to CUPHEAD 1, HILDA 0.

From there, it was all downhill—literally. Hilda

plunged out of the cloud and down to the ground, where she made several uncomfortable-looking bounces across the schoolyard. She wasn't badly hurt, thank goodness, but Cuphead, who was watching from the window, noticed that when she walked away, her balloonish body moved in and out like a floppy accordion.

"I wonder what that's all about," he said.

"No talking, Cuphead," Professor Lucien warned. "Keep your eyes on your work."

Cuphead frowned but picked up his pencil and began writing again. A few seconds later, an airplane made of blue paper landed on his desk. It was from Mugman (who, as you know, was crazy about airplanes).

Be careful, Cuphead! the note said. *You can't get in trouble today. Remember, we have to get Elder Kettle's birthday present after school.*

Cuphead sighed. He took out a piece of green paper and wrote *I know!*, then folded it into an airplane and sailed it back to Mugman. Before he could even pick up his pencil again, a purple paper airplane arrived.

What are you two fellas talking about? Ms. Chalice's note asked.

So he pulled out a second piece of green paper, and told her. Then there was another blue plane.

Is Ms. Chalice trying to talk you into going to the carnival? Don't listen to her!

And another purple plane.

I would never, ever, ever try to talk you into going to the carnival on Elder Kettle's birthday, Cuphead. It does sound fun, though. Let's go!

And pretty soon the classroom was filled with so many green, blue, and purple planes it looked like a big-city airfield. Cuphead was just about to launch another note when a neatly made yellow airplane fell on his desk. He opened it.

Cuphead. You have detention.

Sincerely,

Professor Lucien

7

NOBODY HERE BUT US DUMMIES

Detention? It couldn't be. Not the *D* word. Not today! Cuphead looked at Ms. Chalice and Mugman. They were each holding a yellow letter of their own.

How could this happen? How could all three of them get detention on the one day they had to get to Porkrind's shop? Cuphead stared at the agonizing note, hoping he'd read it wrong. He hadn't. Elder Kettle's birthday party would be ruined, and it was all his fault.

This was a disaster.

The next few hours crept by like a snail with nowhere to go and several lifetimes to get there. Finally, the bell rang, and everyone burst from their chairs and ran out of the classroom—everyone except Cuphead, Ms. Chalice, and Mugman. They stayed right where they were.

"I'm sorry, but you broke the rules," Professor Lucien said. Still, he couldn't help giving them an understanding smile. "Don't worry, you'll have plenty of time to go to the carnival. I wouldn't make you miss out on all the fun and excitement."

"But—" Cuphead said.

"No buts," said Lucien. "I'll be over here working on an experiment, so just sit there quietly at your desks."

Cuphead slumped forward. He wanted to tell the professor about Elder Kettle's surprise birthday party, and how the whole town had chipped in to buy him a nice present, and why everything depended on them making it to Porkrind's shop by four o'clock. He wanted to tell him they had no interest in fun and excitement and once-in-a-lifetime wonders and weren't even going to the carnival. But it was no use.

When Professor Lucien was working on an experiment, he shut out everything else in the world. Cuphead watched as the brilliant bulb walked to the corner of the room and mixed colorful, strange-looking fluids in his test tubes and beakers. There was no reaching him now. He was lost in a mysterious land called Science.

The three friends pushed their desks close together.

"Jeepers, we sure are in a pickle," Cuphead whispered. "What are we going to do?"

"Maybe we could...uh, sneak out," Mugman whispered back.

"I think he'd notice if he were all alone in an empty room," Cuphead said.

Suddenly, Professor Lucien looked up at them.

"Did you say something?" he asked.

The three of them smiled innocently and shook their heads. He went back to his experiment.

"Well, what if he wasn't alone?" Ms. Chalice said.

The boys looked confused.

"Who'd be here with him?" said Cuphead.

"We would," she said.

They looked even more confused.

"I'll show you." She grinned.

Stealthily, Ms. Chalice slipped out of her desk like butter sliding off a pancake. In the blink of an eye, she blazed around the room grabbing as many items as she could carry, then rushed back and sat down in her proper place.

It's a good thing she returned when she did. Because no sooner had she sat down in her chair than

Professor Lucien stopped his experiment and gave them a long, probing stare. But just as before, all he saw were three perfect angels smiling back at him. He raised an eyebrow (which, as anyone will tell you, is a sure sign of suspicion), but quickly put it down and went on with his work.

"Whew! That was close," Ms. Chalice said.

She pulled out the spoils of her collecting spree. There was a flower vase, a yardstick, a mop, a seat cushion, two paintbrushes, books of various colors and sizes, and an assortment of odds and ends that had been permanently left in the lost and found because no one wanted them back. Working at incredible speed (Ms. Chalice had many talents, but she was especially good at art), she fashioned a bizarre figure out of the materials and sat it in her chair.

Cuphead and Mugman stared at the creation. The resemblance was . . . actually, there was no resemblance. It looked like a monster made entirely of school supplies had wandered into the classroom, swallowed Ms. Chalice, and taken her place in the desk.

"You've got to be kidding," Cuphead groaned.

The professor looked up. This time, he really was

suspicious. Ms. Chalice quickly ducked down behind her double.

"Are you feeling all right, Ms. Chalice?"

There was a long, uncomfortable silence. This was unbearable. Now he wasn't just looking at the horrible mess, he was asking it questions!

"I'm as fit as a fiddle, Professor," she said at last.

The next few seconds were excruciating. Lucien scratched the side of his bulb, then he scratched the other side, and then—for reasons only someone of his profound intellect could understand—he went back to his experiment.

"I can't believe that worked," said Mugman.

"I told you it would," Ms. Chalice said. "Once he starts on an experiment, he doesn't pay the slightest bit of attention to anything else. So get busy."

Mugman and Cuphead eased out of their desks and wriggled across the floor like worms. They returned with a janitor's bucket, construction paper, a broom, a classroom pointer, a round light fixture, a football, and various doodads (the isles were famous for their doodads) that they fashioned into hideous facsimiles of themselves.

"It's like looking in a mirror," Mugman said. "Except there's someone completely different looking back at you."

They almost burst out laughing. It was a ridiculous plan, but what else could they do? They put the dummies in place and were sneaking away as quietly as possible when, just as they reached the window, Lucien (who seemed determined to make this escape as difficult as possible) sneezed.

"Gesundheit," said Cuphead.

It was a reflex, the kind of thing any well-brought-up boy would do, and so he said it without thinking. Ms. Chalice slapped a hand over his mouth, but by then it was too late. They dived behind their desks just as the professor looked their way.

"What's that, Cuphead? If you wish to speak, raise your hand," he said.

But Cuphead did not wish to speak. He wished he'd never spoken, and there was no way in the world he was going to speak again—but he had to. After all, it was only polite. So he carefully pushed up one of the clunky yardstick-arms and it rose slowly into the air.

"Um, I said," he said nervously, "gesundheit."

"Oh. Thank you, Cuphead," Lucien said, and went back to work.

At that moment, a small, cheerful-looking, red figure strolled into the room. It was their classmate Mac.

"Howdy," he said brightly. "I finished dusting the erasers."

Of course, no one had asked him to dust the erasers, but he'd done it anyway. That was Mac, as helpful a little apple as you'd ever want to meet. He was always ready to lend a hand.

"Just put them by the chalkboard, Mac," the professor said.

Ms. Chalice's eyes brightened. She couldn't believe their luck. "I've got an idea!" she said.

She wiggled a finger at Mac. He smiled and made his way to the group.

"Howdy," said he said again.

"Mac, do you think you can put on a puppet show?" Ms. Chalice whispered.

Mac's face lit up.

"Can I?!" he exclaimed, and pulled out a pair of sock puppets he kept around for just such an occasion.

"No, I didn't mean—" Ms. Chalice tried to tell him, but he was too excited to notice.

"What do you get when you cross a parrot with a crocodile?" one puppet asked.

"I don't know, but when it talks, you better listen!" said the other.

"*Shhhhhhh!*" Cuphead told him. "It's not that kind of puppet show. We just want you to wiggle these dummies around whenever the professor looks over here."

"Well, why didn't you say so?" Mac said. "It's a piece of cake!"

Mugman appreciated Mac's enthusiasm, but he couldn't help being concerned. It was a big job for a little apple.

"Now, only move them if he turns around. Don't go overboard, okay?"

"Don't worry, it'll be a cinch," Mac said.

So with their fears put to rest, the three friends headed back toward the window. But just before they crawled outside, they heard a peculiar voice.

"Oh Per-fessor! Per-fessor!"

It was coming from behind Cuphead's chair. And Mac was making it.

At first, they couldn't figure out what he was doing. Then, to their horror, they realized it was a terrible, terrible impression of Cuphead. It sounded like a scratchy record with a bad cold. The trio hit the floor just before the professor wheeled around.

"What is it now, Cuphead?" Lucien asked.

"Per-fessor, I was wonderin' if you'd like to hear a song?" the fake Cuphead said.

"No!" Cuphead whisper-screamed, but Mac ignored him.

"What kind of song?" asked the professor.

"*Row, row, row your boat, gently down the stream,*" the apple started. His co-conspirators buried their faces in their hands, silently begging him to stop. But he didn't. Instead, he quickly moved to the Ms. Chalice and Mugman dolls, who joined in on the chorus.

"*Merrily, merrily, merrily, merrily, life is but a dream!*"

And that wasn't all. There was swaying and clapping and a brief dance number that had to be seen to be believed. Mac flew like a wizard from dummy to dummy, sometimes doing two, even three voices at a time. It was horrifying, yet oddly impressive.

Cuphead knew they were done for. He just knew

it. The punishment was coming, and it would be swift and severe. But just when he was about to surrender and admit the whole thing—

"Very nice," said the professor. "But I'm busy right now, Cuphead. Perhaps we can do this later."

Wait . . . he was buying this? Cuphead and Mugman stared at Ms. Chalice. She shrugged.

"What can I tell you? The kid's a natural showman," she said.

They shook their heads and made their way to the window. Nothing could stop them now. And yet Ms. Chalice did.

"Oh my gosh!" she said, then rushed back to her desk. Once there, she picked up a red crayon and colored in the round, white knob that served as Counterfeit Cuphead's nose.

"A perfect match." She grinned. "I can't believe we almost missed that. Why it was as plain as the nose on your—"

But before she could finish the thought, Cuphead yanked her away to the window, and as quickly and quietly as they could, the trio slipped out the window, shimmied down the drainpipe, and were on their way.

8
IN A PICKLE AT PORKRIND'S

They hit the ground running, which isn't easy, but that's what you do when there isn't a moment to spare. Side by side by side, the trio raced into town, their legs spinning like tiny whirlwinds. In practically no time at all, they'd left the countryside behind and were within striking distance of their destination. They rounded the last corner, streaked down the sidewalk, and at maximum speed, burst through the door of Porkrind's shop. It was a heroic entrance—or would've been if Porkrind hadn't just finished mopping the floor.

They skidded, headfirst, into the pickle barrel.

"You got two minutes," the shopkeeper grunted.

Now, if you've never run the long stretch from the schoolhouse to Porkrind's at top speed without a single break, you might think two minutes was plenty of time. But you would be wrong. The truth is, for several precious seconds, Cuphead did nothing but stand there panting and gasping and squeezing pickle juice out of his nostrils. But when he finally did manage to catch his breath, he immediately wheezed out, "That's hunky-dory (*pant*), because all we (*pant*) want is—"

"This airplane," Mugman said.

Cuphead whirled around and saw his brother holding one of the models he'd been looking at earlier that day. It was a real beauty, the kind with a propeller that spun when you wound up the rubber band.

"We don't want an airplane!" Cuphead barked. "This is for Elder Kettle. We want—"

"*Ooh*, did you see this fancy can opener?" said Ms. Chalice. "Holy moly, those cans wouldn't stand a chance!"

"No, no, no!" Cuphead said. "We came for the watch, remember?"

"Oh yeah," Mugman said. "Elder Kettle could use a nice watch."

Porkrind grumped and grumbled, but finally bent over and pulled the watch out of the case beneath the cash register. Cuphead beamed. It was even more perfect than he remembered. He quickly pulled a big wad of bills and coins out of his pocket and plopped it on the counter. It was all the money that Elder

Kettle's friends had pooled together, and it made an impressive pile.

Porkrind just stared at it.

"You're short," he said.

Short? What? But how? Oh no! Instantly, Mugman and Ms. Chalice pulled money out of their own pockets and placed it on the counter. Porkrind looked at it as he twisted the toothpick hanging from the corner of his mouth.

"Still short," he said.

This was getting serious. They yanked their pockets inside out but found nothing. Then they took off their shoes and emptied them. Still nothing. Finally, Cuphead and Ms. Chalice picked up Mugman, turned him topsy-turvy, and bobbed him up and down like a butter churn. Several coins fell out of his straw.

"I wondered where I put those," Mugman said.

Hurriedly, they slammed the coins on the counter while Porkrind stared at the clock on the wall.

"You're still a nickel short," he said, grinning. "And I close in exactly one minute."

Now Cuphead was frantic. He reached deep into his pocket, then through a hole in the pocket, and finally through a hole in the hole, which led to a place called

Pocket Town. It was a nice little town filled with nice little people made of lint. They'd tip their hats and nod politely whenever you met them on Pocket Street or at the lint-brary, because life was "a *hole* lot simpler here." (This was the funniest joke in Pocket Town, and they never got tired of telling it.) Cuphead's fingers strolled past several pocket shops and establishments until they came to a small, neat building with a sign out front. It said POCKET BANK. They walked inside, where they waited behind a velvet rope until the lint-teller called them forward. After a warm greeting and the telling of the town joke (they're called *tellers* for a reason, you know), he handed the fingers a shiny new nickel.

Cuphead quickly yanked the magnificent coin out of his pocket and held it up in triumph. Mugman and Ms. Chalice cheered. The watch was theirs! The party was saved! But just as Cuphead was about to slap the glimmering nickel down on the counter—

"We're closed," Porkrind said.

Without another word, he put the watch back under the counter, shoved the money back in their hands, and pushed the three of them out the door.

"Come back tomorrow," he said.

The door slammed behind them, and as it did, the sign in the window turned from OPEN to CLOSED.

"What are we going to do now?" Mugman groaned.

Cuphead shook his head. He was wondering the same thing himself.

They slumped down into a big, glum heap on the curb, feeling sorry for themselves, and even sorrier for Elder Kettle. This was not at all how things were supposed to go. Cuphead let out a slow, defeated sigh.

And that's when he heard it—a kind of a rinky-tinky noise. It was happy and sad at the same time, and sounded a little like music, only clankier. The more he listened, the catchier it seemed. And it was coming from the other side of the square.

9

A CUPFUL OF TROUBLE

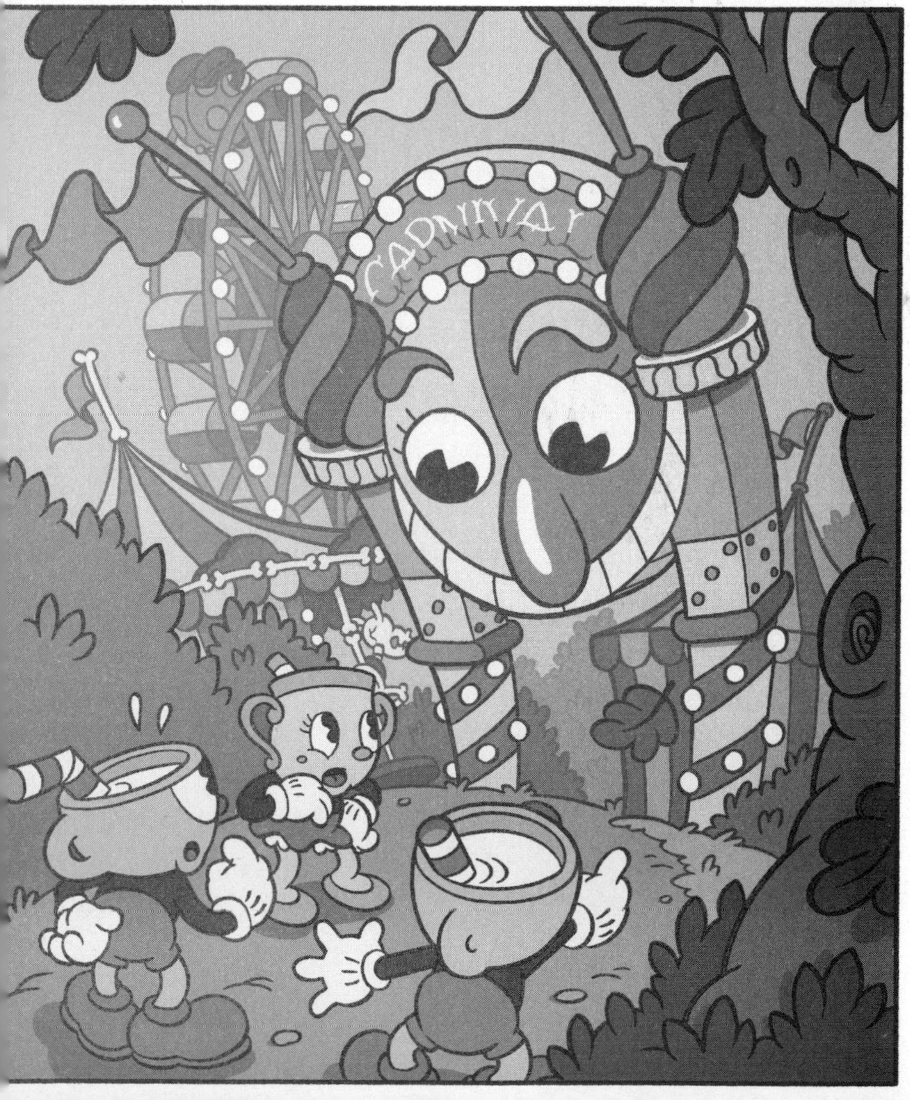

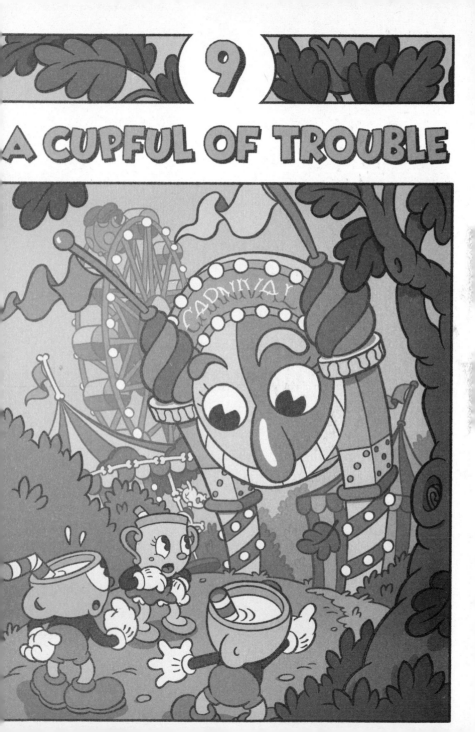

Cuphead, Mugman, and Ms. Chalice walked slowly toward the strange music. Now that they'd gotten used to it, it wasn't nearly as horrible as it sounded at first. In fact, it was mesmerizing—almost irresistible. Before long, Cuphead realized it was leading them back to the exact place where he and Mugman had seen the group of people gathered that morning. But now the crowd was bigger and louder and much more excited.

"What's all the hubbub, bub?" he asked a man in a porkpie hat.

"We're watching Mr. Chimes," said the man. "He plays the street organ."

The three friends peered through the crowd. What they saw was a windup monkey with hollow eyes and an unsettling smile. Strapped to his back was a fancy-looking box that had big brass pipes sticking out of it. Every now and then, the pipes would cough out little puffs of steam, and when they did, it made a musical toot. Meanwhile, Mr. Chimes banged two shiny cymbals together as if he were trying to bash an invisible mosquito.

Ms. Chalice shuddered.

"If you ask me, that monkey's bananas," she said. "I wouldn't want to cross paths with him."

But Cuphead wasn't listening, and he wasn't looking at Mr. Chimes. He was looking at what was behind Mr. Chimes. It was a gate with a wide, arching entrance and a colorful sign that said CARNIVAL.

"Wow!" Cuphead gasped. "So *THAT'S* the carnival."

It was nothing like he'd expected, and not at all like Elder Kettle had described. Cuphead sniffed the air. The scents of every kind of food came together at once and danced in his nostrils. When he stood on his tiptoes, he saw wonders that he couldn't have imagined. There were gigantic tents, and rows of booths and rides—oh, the rides! He saw spinning rides and jumping rides and flying rides and bumping rides. They looked absolutely thrilling and without any of the annoying deadliness that came with a roller coaster. In fact, Cuphead was so taken with the place that he forgot all about that mechanical monstrosity and, for the first time, saw the carnival for what it was—a tiny city devoted to fun.

"Let's go in!" he said, and boldly walked toward the gate.

At least he tried to walk. His legs were moving, but his feet weren't touching the ground. That's because Mugman had lifted him into the air and was carrying him in the opposite direction.

"Did you forget what we promised Elder Kettle?" he asked.

"I'm trying to, but you keep reminding me!" wailed Cuphead.

Mugman carried his brother over to the sidewalk and dropped him there. Then he shook his head and made a disappointed noise, the one that sounds like a chipmunk with something stuck on its gums.

"Cuphead, that's the carnival. You know what Elder Kettle said. It's a vile, evil place and we promised him we wouldn't go," he scolded, then crossed his arms and turned his back. "But if you want to break Elder Kettle's heart, I won't stop you."

"Great!" Cuphead said, and dashed off for the gate again.

But he didn't get far. How could he? Before he'd

even taken two steps, Mugman's words were echoing through his brain. They were true, of course. It would break Elder Kettle's heart. He kicked at the ground. Oh, this was agony! He wanted to keep his promise, he really did. But the carnival was right there! Was he supposed to just walk away from what might be the experience of a lifetime?

It was a dilemma, all right. A big one. Fortunately, there was someone he could always turn to for guidance, and at that moment, a very small cup, identical to him in almost every way, appeared out of nowhere. It had little wings, and a shiny halo around its straw, and it hovered just above his right shoulder.

This was Cuphead's conscience.

"Cuphead, listen to your heart," his conscience told him. "There's nothing inside those gates as valuable as Elder Kettle's trust."

POOF!

"What a dum-dum!" said another tiny cup that appeared over his left shoulder. This one had horns and a pronged tail. "Take a good long whiff, pal. Did you ever smell anything like that in your life? Forget about Elder Kettle—just follow your nose to the land of forbidden temptations!"

"Cuphead," said Good Cuphead. "He's trying to lead you to ruin."

"Ruin, schmuin. Don't be a sucker, get in there!" the other cup snickered.

Cuphead thought they both made strong points. He listened intently and as they argued, his pupils darted back and forth like they were watching a ping-pong match. It was exhausting. Finally, he closed his eyes and wished they'd both just go away.

But it wasn't that easy. When he opened them again, they were still there. Only now, the good one was holding something white and fluffy.

"Is that cotton candy?" Cuphead asked.

"Don't change the subject," the cup snapped back. "This is about you."

Well, that started the two tiny cups arguing all over again, and it might have gone on for hours had Ms. Chalice not stepped in and waved them both away. Then she put her hand on Cuphead's shoulder.

"You know, Cuphead, I wanted to go in there as much as anybody. But there will be other carnivals," she said. "Right now, what we've really got to worry about is Elder Kettle's birthday present. If we don't get that blah, blah, blah..."

Of course, she didn't actually say "blah, blah, blah," but that's what you would've heard if you'd been there. You see, your attention at that moment would've been pulled to something much more interesting happening just a few feet away. Mugman's eyes, which almost never did anything un-eyelike, had started to spin like two hypnotic pinwheels. Also, his heart was springing in and out of his chest like a paddleball. It was an unusual look for Mugman (who prided himself on his well-behaved organs), and why it was happening was a complete mystery—until you followed his gaze all the way to the carnival gate.

That's where you'd find her—Cala Maria. She was known far and wide as the most beautiful creature on the Inkwell Isles. She had big, sparkly eyes and a captivating smile, and was in every way the very picture of what you'd expect a mermaid to be. She winked at Mugman, and little hearts bubbled out of his straw. When she blew him a kiss, his cheeks blushed so red you'd have sworn he was breaking out in tomatoes.

Now, you mustn't blame Mugman for what happened next. It was entirely out of his control. One minute he was standing there as upright as can be, and the next his feet were off the ground and he was floating gently through the air. This has happened only twice before in the whole history of the isles: once when Tubby O'Toole was levitated by the aroma of a freshly baked pie; and again, when a lullaby carried a very sleepy bear home just in time for hibernation. As you can see, it was extremely rare, and never, ever had it happened on the strength of an airborne kiss, which gives you some idea of Cala Maria's power over Mugman.

In the end, he blissfully floated right through the crowd, and it was only by sheer luck that Ms. Chalice spotted Mugman as he was entering the gate.

"We've got to stop him!" she cried.

She grabbed Cuphead by the hand and they pushed and prodded their way through the crowd. But by the time they got to the gate, Mugman had disappeared. They were just about to go inside when a large flower with bulgy eyes and a bad disposition stopped them.

"Hey, you two," Cagney Carnation said. "What's the big idea?"

"My brother just went through this gate," Cuphead told him, "and we've got to go after him."

"You ain't goin' nowhere without a ticket, see?

Those is the rules," Cagney said, and he flicked his toothpick into Cuphead's head.

Cuphead didn't like being used as a waste bin. He also didn't like being kept outside while his brother was floating off to who knows where. But buying a ticket? That would be spending money they needed for Elder Kettle's gift. He looked at Ms. Chalice.

"I don't think we have a choice," she said.

Cuphead didn't, either. He thought for a moment, then looked at Cagney.

"Two tickets, please," he said.

10

OH BROTHER, WHERE ART THOU?

They paid the carnation and rushed through the gate.

"Mugman!" Cuphead yelled. "*MUGGGGGGG*-man!"

He was nowhere to be found. They looked up and down and side to side, but it was hopeless. Mugman had simply vanished. He could be anywhere, and *anywhere* covered an awful lot of territory. Cuphead whirled around, marveling at the massive carnival grounds—and that's when he realized something. He was hungry—really hungry—and it's no wonder. Wherever he turned, there were aisles and aisles of vendors selling exotic delicacies from around the world, and all of them came on a stick. If that wasn't distracting enough, there were tents and rides and games as far as the eye could see. But mostly, there were people. Lots and lots of people. This wouldn't be easy.

"Any luck?" Ms. Chalice asked.

Cuphead shook his head.

"Well, keep trying. I'll go look over here," she said.

A second later, she was swallowed up by the crowd, and Cuphead wondered how they were ever going to find one little mug in a place like this. They couldn't do it alone, that was for sure. Maybe someone who worked here could help them. He wandered around looking for a carnival professional who specialized in finding lost children, but he didn't see one. Finally, he spotted a tall figure in a fancy costume who was juggling six yellow balls in the air. His back was turned, so Cuphead couldn't see his face, but he was tired of looking, and had decided one employee would be as good as another.

"Hey, mister," Cuphead said, tugging on the man's sleeve. "Have you seen my—"

The man turned around. Suddenly, Cuphead felt the blood freeze in his veins. Within seconds, his whole body had stiffened into a cup-sicle. The stranger's face was painted like a clown, but with an eerie, evil grin. Cuphead had always found clowns a little scary, and after Elder Kettle's story that morning, the last thing he wanted was to be face-to-face with one. Especially not when the face looked like this.

"I'm Beppi the Clown," the painted man said. "Don't be afraid. Everybody loves a clown."

Then his twisted face broke into an even more twisted smile.

"What can I do for you, sonny?" he said, but Cuphead was too frozen to speak.

"Cat got your tongue?" he asked, pulling a cat from his pocket. The cat then opened a small suitcase like a door-to-door salesman, displaying a wide selection of tongues.

But still, Cuphead said nothing. The clown scratched his head.

"Balloon animal? Juggling show? Jokes? Pratfalls? Pie in the face?"

As he listed his various clown skills, Beppi bounced about the pathway flinging objects from his pockets and doing cartwheels and handsprings and somersaults. It was amusing in a maniacal sort of way. But what wasn't amusing, not in any way, was the laugh that burst out of him. Cuphead thought it the most menacing thing he'd ever heard.

Beppi stared at him and cocked his head to one side.

"So what's it going to be, sonny? Oh wait, I know!" he quipped, and then came the words Cuphead feared most of all. "Guess your weight?"

The question seemed to pour out in slow motion, and the world around them grew dark and distant. But Cuphead was too stunned to move. Beppi's rubbery arms reached down for him, those abominable fingers readying for the clutch—

And that's when Ms. Chalice stepped in the way.

"How 'bout guessin' my weight?" she said cheerfully.

At first, Beppi looked irritated. But then the twisted smile returned.

"Be glad to, little lady," he oozed.

With all the care of a berserk baggage handler, he grabbed her by the shoulders and lifted her into the air. Then he started to shake, and shake, and—

KLANGGGGG!

An anvil fell on Beppi's head. Instantly, a lump the size of a cucumber sprouted from his skull, and little stars whirled round it like a maypole.

"Oops. It looks like I put on a little weight," Ms. Chalice said.

Then, as if it were just another day at the carnival, she grabbed Cuphead by the hand and dragged him down the path.

"Well, where to from here?" she asked.

"Beats me," Cuphead said, and he looked around for any sign of Mugman.

There was nothing. But just then, four balloons drifted down from the sky and hovered in front of them. One by one, they popped, leaving in their place four friendly-looking fellows with long, thin, striped bodies.

"*Helloooooooo!*"

"*Helloooooooo!*"

"*Helloooooooo!*"

"*Helloooooooooo!*" they harmonized.

"Who are you?" Cuphead asked.

They introduced themselves. Their names were Mel, Melvin, Melroy, and Melbert.

"They're the Four Mel Arrangement. I've heard of them," Ms. Chalice said.

The Mels were a barbershop quartet and, like all barbershop quartets, they preferred to communicate in song. So, after clearing their throats and tooting

their pitch pipe, they crooned a snappy little ditty that
went something like this:

> *If you* REAL-LY *want to* FIND *your friend—*
> *(Bom, bom, bom, bom)*
> *So you all can be* TO-GETH-ER *again—*
> *(Bom, bom, bom, bom)*
> *Stop look-ing* THIS *way, when you should look* THAT—
> *(Bom, bom, bom, bom)*
> *'Cuz that won't get you where your* BROTHER *is* AT—
> *(Bom, bom, bom,* BOM *)*
> *Now he's been* SPOT-TED *with Cala* MARIA—
> *(Bom, bom, bom, bom)*
> *And when you* FIND *him he'll be* HAPPY *to see ya—*
> (AHHHHHHHHHHH–)
> *But* BE-*fore you go and* QUES-*tion every* LA-DY *and*
>   GENT—
> (BOM, BOM, BOM, BOM)
> *If we were you we'd take a peek inside that*
>   tennnnnnnnnnnt!

And then, as all great artists do, the four Mels filled
their heads with air and floated away like balloons. (It's
always better to leave your audience wanting more.)

Unfortunately, their abrupt departure left no time to answer one simple question.

"Which tent?" Ms. Chalice asked.

In fact, there were tents everywhere. When Cuphead looked down the aisle, he saw rows and rows and rows of tents exactly like the one he saw going up that morning. And Mugman could be in any of them. Or none of them. It would've been nice if the Mels had been a little more specific.

Still, it was something. And since they had to start somewhere, they headed to the closest one. Outside it, a zebra with a cane and a straw hat was standing on an upside-down soapbox.

"Hurry, hurry, step right up," said the zebra. "Come experience the most stupendous, stupefying, unforgettable exhibition ever brought to these shores. See the greatest actress of our age live and onstage performing dramatic deeds of diction that will dazzle and delight you. Your entrance to this exquisite enter-tainment extravaganza is right through that golden gateway. No need to push, folks, there's always room in the back. Hurry, hurry, don't be shy."

"Excuse me, sir," Cuphead said. "Did you see a mug and a mermaid go inside?"

The zebra leaned over.

"I see a lot of mugs and a lot of mermaids, kid," he said. "Maybe they went in, maybe they didn't. Say, why don't you go inside and see for yourself?"

He tapped his cane on a sign that said 25 CENTS and stuck out his hand. Cuphead and Ms. Chalice shrugged, and each held out a quarter.

The next thing they knew, they were headed inside to see Sally Stageplay, the most famous actress they'd *never* heard of.

• • • • •

The first thing they noticed was that the tent was crowded. The second thing was that it was dark.

"We'll never find him in this tomb. I can't see my hand in front of my face," said Ms. Chalice.

It was true. When she raised her hand, all she saw was the end of her long black sleeve. Cuphead looked at her, rolled his eyes, and squeezed the sleeve like a toothpaste tube. A white glove popped out.

"Oh, there it is." She smiled.

Cuphead was annoyed. They didn't have time for this nonsense. Still, Ms. Chalice had a point—it was darker than a groundhog's basement in here. They wouldn't spot Mugman if he were standing right next to them. They really wouldn't.

"Are you Mugman?" Ms. Chalice asked the figure right next to her.

"No, I'm Carl."

"But you'd tell me if you were Mugman?"

"Yes. But I'm not."

"I see," she said. "This has been a disappointing conversation, Carl."

The search was getting them nowhere.

"There's some light over there," Cuphead told her, pointing to a raised platform that had lamps all around it. "Let's go."

Of course, getting there was easier said than done. The tent was packed with Sally Stageplay supporters, and for twenty-five cents, they expected their experience to be up close and Sally-ful. That didn't worry Cuphead—he wasn't about to let a bunch of footlight flunkies keep him at the back of the tent. He and Ms. Chalice lowered their shoulders and, with a mighty thrust, pushed and shoved and prodded their way to exactly where they started.

"Well, that was pointless," said Ms. Chalice.

She was right, but it was hardly their fault. They were up against the great wall of drama, an impenetrable barrier made entirely of theater fans. The path to the stage was a jungle of elbows and knees and hip bones jammed so tightly together it was a wonder anyone could breathe. It was a frustrating situation, and practically anyone else would've raised a fuss, but Cuphead and Ms. Chalice decided to take the high road.

"Sorry. Comin' through. 'Scuse me. Love your hat. 'Scuse me," Ms. Chalice said as the two of them stepped from head to head to head. In no time at all, they had walked across the top of the crowd and strolled right onto the stage.

The light was considerably better here, but try as he might, Cuphead still couldn't make out faces. He picked up one of the lamps at the edge of the stage and held it out above the crowd.

"Mugman!" he called. "*MUG*-man!"

"Hey, down in front!" an angry voice yelled, and that's when Cuphead and Ms. Chalice felt several burly hands grab hold and yank them down into the darkness.

Well, this was a fine how-do-you-do. After all, they

were paying customers. Cuphead had a good mind to go speak to the manager, but before he could even turn himself around, the whole place got deathly still.

When he looked up, Sally Stageplay was standing right in front of him.

"*Romee-ohh*, oh *Romee-ohh*, et ceter-*AH*, et ceter-*AH*, et ceter-*AH*," she intoned.

The crowd gasped. Then cried. Then cheered! They couldn't believe what they were witnessing. She trod the boards until they were splinters! She chewed the scenery like a magnificent gumball! The audience was spellbound as she enunciated and articulated and emoted and swooned. Finally, after her twenty-seventh encore (in the interest of time, Sally skipped performances and went straight to encores), she put her wrist against her forehead, groaned loudly, and—*SPROING!*—made her body stiff as an ironing board. It lingered in the air for a heartbreaking instant, then plopped onto the stage. And just when her fans thought they'd seen the greatest death scene that could ever be performed—

POP!

A rubber lily sprung up from her chest-crossed hands.

The room exploded in a roaring ovation. Sally immediately rose to her feet and took several long, humble bows as Cuphead and Ms. Chalice looked on in awe. It was an amazing performance—but not as amazing as the one happening right under their noses.

You see, as good as Sally was at ACTING, she was even better at distrACTING. While the audience cheered, her supporting cast (a group of adorably malicious cherubs) roamed through the crowd pilfering purses and waylaying wallets. In the meantime, Sally—while taking a *verrrrrrrry* deep bow—reached down and lifted several bills from Ms. Chalice's pocket.

Elder Kettle was right. The carnival was a place of liars and thieves.

As the curtain fell, the entire cast gathered onstage to soak in the applause (and stuff the loot into Sally's parasol). But just then, the spotlight at the top of the tent—which ordinarily stuck to Sally like an ugly rumor—moved away from the star and onto the audience.

"*MUG*-man!" yelled Cuphead, shining the bright beam on the crowd. "*MUUUUUUUUG*-man!"

Sally's eyes shot up. She was furious.

"What are you doing up there?" she seethed. "I demand you give me my spotlight!"

"But I was just—"

"I want my spotlight, and I want it now!" she bellowed.

Oh dear. Cuphead hadn't meant to upset Sally; he'd just wanted to find Mugman. He needed to fix this.

"Whatever you say," he said, and tossed the gargantuan light onto the stage.

This was not what Sally had in mind. The spotlight hit the boards like a meteor, catapulting her and her treacherous troupe into the air and out over the crowd. It was a very dramatic moment. But not as dramatic as the moment her parasol popped open, raining coins and jewelry and wallets on the audience below. Needless to say, this caused quite a commotion, but Cuphead and Ms. Chalice never saw a bit of it.

By the time the scene played out, they were already on their way out of the tent, back on the trail of the missing Mugman. Sally's autograph would have to wait for another day.

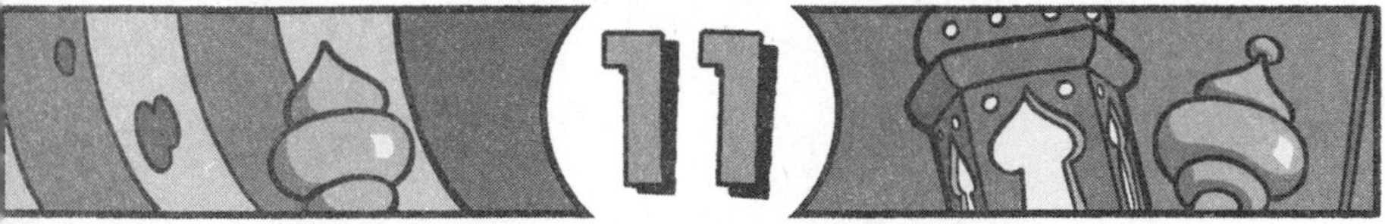
11

DJUMPIN' DJIMMINI!

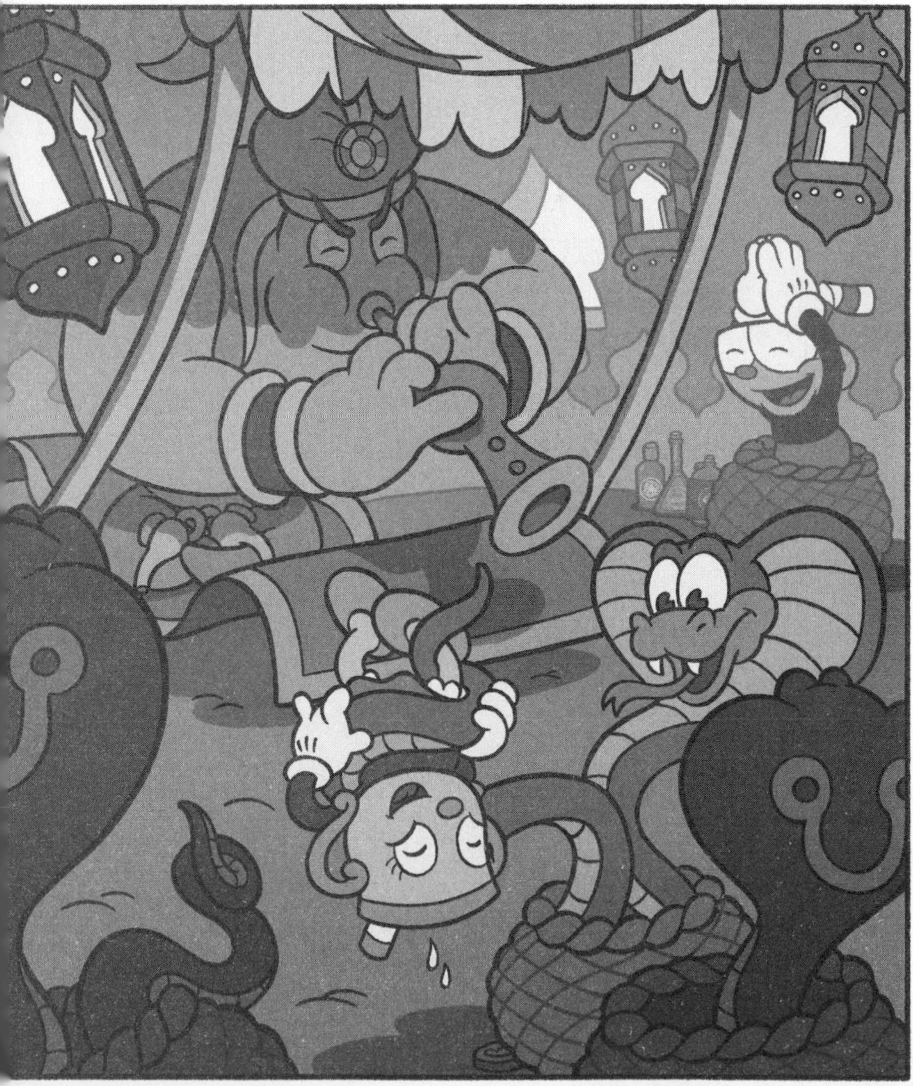

There was only one thing to do—go on to the next tent. Luckily, it was just on the other side of the aisle. This one looked almost identical to the last one, except it had exotic flags out front and a large banner that said DJIMMI THE GREAT, WONDER OF THE EAST. MIRACLES. MAGIC. CURLY FRIES.

"We can't go in," Cuphead said. "It's twenty-five cents admission, and we've spent too much already. That money's for Elder Kettle's birthday present."

It was a quandary all right, and it had been weighing on him since the moment they'd arrived. Ms. Chalice gave him a sympathetic smile.

"I know, but we have to go in there, Cuphead. Mugman could be in real trouble," she told him. "Also, they have curly fries."

Cuphead nodded, but still wasn't convinced. He didn't feel right about spending other people's money.

On the other hand, the sign did say Djimmi the Great performed miracles—and boy oh boy, could they use a miracle.

Unfortunately, a fez-wearing camel stood between them and the entrance. Then a miracle *did* happen. A beret-wearing camel offered the fez-wearing camel a glass of water, which allowed Cuphead and Ms. Chalice to tiptoe past them without paying a dime. Or even two quarters.

On the inside, this tent was nothing at all like Sally Stageplay's. It was a wonderland of rugs and pillows and lanterns and silks. In the very center of the stage was an oil lamp that looked a little like a teapot, and there were decorative baskets of various shapes and sizes all around it. Finally, towering above everything else were two gigantic, golden swords that came together to form a gleaming archway. Cuphead was enthralled.

"Do you see him?" Ms. Chalice asked.

"No, he's probably still backstage."

"I meant *Mugman*," she said.

Cuphead turned fire-engine red.

"Oh yeah. Mugman," he said. "I was just about to look for him."

The truth was, he'd forgotten. He hadn't meant to; it's just that this place was so . . . *incredible*! Even though he knew they had to find Mugman, he couldn't help being excited. This was different from anything he'd ever seen on the Inkwell Isles. It was like a weird, wonderful dream that charged you twenty-five cents to have it.

Suddenly, the lights in the room dimmed, and from out of the lamp there came a flash of fire and a puff of orange smoke. When the smoke cleared, Djimmi the Great was standing there on the stage! The audience, led by an ecstatic Cuphead, burst into wild applause.

What an entrance! If the rest of the show was half this spectacular, Cuphead was in for the thrill of his life. The only thing bothering him was an irritating tapping on his right shoulder. It was very persistent. He ignored it for as long as he could, hoping it would just go away. But it didn't. And it wouldn't. And he knew why. Finally, he turned and looked.

Good Cuphead was back—and shaking his head disapprovingly. Bad Cuphead was back, too, but he just winked and whistled and pointed to the stage.

The sight of the two of them gave Cuphead a sad, sickly feeling in his stomach. He leaned in close to Ms. Chalice.

"I know we're here looking for Mugman," he whispered. "But if we watch the show, isn't that like stealing?"

"Only if we're entertained," Ms. Chalice whispered back. "We can watch as much as we want as long as we don't enjoy it."

As usual, Ms. Chalice was a fountain of wisdom. Still, it wasn't going to be easy. Because what was happening up on that stage was as entertaining as anything Cuphead had ever seen.

Djimmi the Great was a powerful genie with a turquoise turban and a magic carpet. He told fortunes. He ate fire. He turned himself into an elephant and then an alligator and then an elegator (which was an alligator with the head of an elephant) and finally a pop-up toaster.

"And now, my friends, I shall perform my most remarkable feat," Djimmi announced. "I shall charm the deadliest creature on the seven continents—the venomous cobra!"

Then, from out of thin air, he conjured a long,

slender pipe. It wasn't the smoking kind of pipe, or the kind that attaches to sinks or toilets or radiators. This was a musical pipe, and Djimmi lifted it to his lips and began to play a strange, haunting tune. Well, that was impressive enough, but it was only the beginning. From the baskets on each side of him, two large snakes appeared. They rose slowly upward, moving rhythmically to the sound of the music. As far as Cuphead could tell, they were completely hypnotized, which he found absolutely astonishing (of all the things he'd ever seen done with a magical pipe, a basket, and a couple of snakes, this was by far the best). But what he didn't know was that the snakes weren't the only ones being charmed. Without realizing it, Cuphead had begun doing a kind of wiggly, wavy dance. Of course, he was completely unaware of what was happening, which was probably for the best. Because at that very moment, one of the enormous serpents wriggled down from the stage, wrapped itself around him, and slipped its tail into his pocket. Then, with the grace of a cat burglar (which isn't easy for a snake burglar), it snatched Elder Kettle's birthday gift money, and made a sinister, slithering retreat to the basket.

Now, it would be one thing if this were the work of a

single snake (who may have had an unhappy childhood or gotten in with the wrong crowd), but it was worse than that. You see, there were other snakes in the tent during that performance, picking the pockets of other wiggly, wavy dancers. Where they came from is anyone's guess, but there's no doubt who was behind it all. At Djimmi's musical command, the slithery gang turned, brought their treacherous take to the stage, and deposited it into the decorative baskets of various shapes and sizes.

Elder Kettle's warning about the carnival was proving more and more correct.

When the last snake had slinked away, Djimmi put down his pipe and took a low, grateful bow. The audience snapped out of its trance just in time to deliver a thunderous round of applause. As for Cuphead, he thought the show was spectacular. He couldn't wait to tell Mugman.

Mugman!

"We've got to get going!" he cried.

But they weren't going anywhere. The tent was packed with spectators, and it would take forever to get through them. Cuphead looked around.

"Follow me," he told Ms. Chalice.

The two of them climbed onto the stage, hoping to get out the back way. Instead, they were stopped dead in their tracks.

Genies, it turns out, are touchy about having their performances interrupted, and Djimmi was no exception. No sooner had Cuphead and Ms. Chalice stepped onstage than the two giant, golden swords that towered above everything else swooped down and formed a barrier in front of them. But that wasn't the worst part. The worst part was when the blades moved forward, sharpening each other like carving knives before a turkey dinner.

Cuphead gulped. He hadn't expected magical swords, and sweat flowed from his cup like an overfilled bathtub. Still, he wasn't one to run from a fight. Summoning his courage, he stepped in front of Ms. Chalice, reached behind his back, and pulled out a sign.

FREE FENCING LESSONS! it said, and there was a big red arrow pointing to the exit.

Instantly, the swords swooshed past them and over to the exhibit hall, where a man in overalls was giving a demonstration on how to build a picket fence. They were captivated.

"Boy, swords sure are crazy about building fences," said Ms. Chalice.

And with that, they were off again.

Fortunately, nothing else happened while they were taking the shortcut to the back of the tent.... Well, there was one little snag. It seems that as they were racing across the stage, Cuphead's straw accidentally caught a loose end dangling from Djimmi's turban. And since Cuphead kept running, the turban kept unrolling and unrolling and unrolling. By the end, Djimmi was twirling around like a magical tornado. He knocked over the rugs and the lamps and the silks and—for a grand finale—the baskets. As you can imagine, the sight of their personal belongings spilling out in a jumble of reptilian robbers caused quite a stir in the audience. Which is why Djimmi decided this would be the perfect time to go into his disappearing act. He bowed, turned himself into a puff of orange smoke, and fled to the safety of his lamp.

Now, if you had wandered in off the street a minute or two later, you might have wondered why an angry mob was standing on the stage kicking an oil lamp around like a soccer ball. Suffice it to say this is what angry mobs do. By the time they finished, the lamp was dented and scratched and generally brutalized, and there's no reason to believe Djimmi made out any better.

12

HIGH HOPES

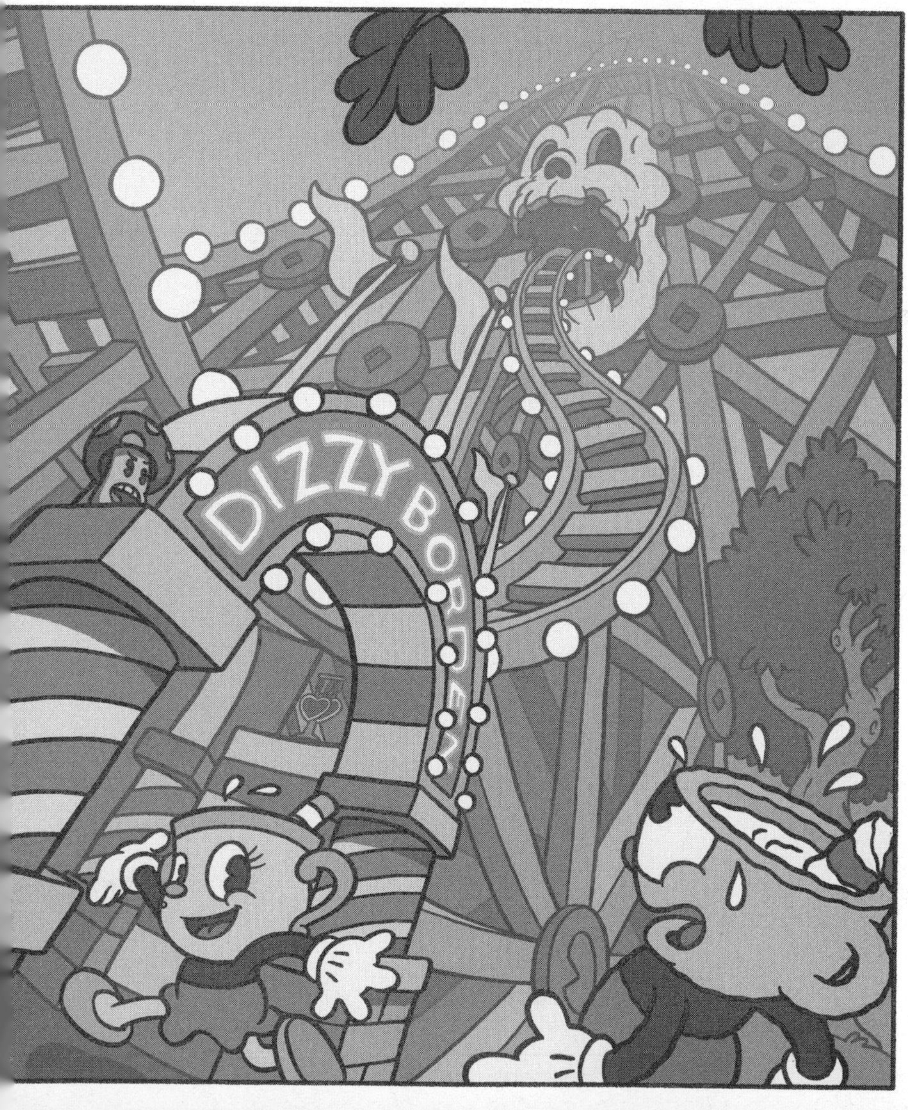
DIZZY

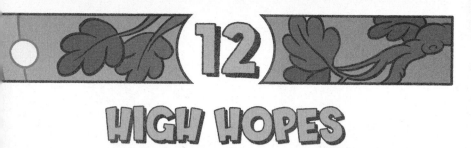

Cuphead pulled loose an annoying strip of cloth that, for some reason, was hanging from his straw.

"Where are we going?" he asked.

"There," said Ms. Chalice.

She pointed to something in the distance. Cuphead couldn't make out exactly what it was, but it looked like a stretch of railroad track an angry giant had tied into a sailor's knot.

"Jeepers, what's that?" he said.

When he looked back at Ms. Chalice, she was grinning from ear to ear.

"That, buddy boy, is the Dizzy Borden," she said excitedly, "the swerviest, curviest, niftiest, swiftiest roller coaster in the whole wide world!"

"Roller coaster?" Cuphead gulped.

Oh dear. He knew there was something about the

carnival he didn't like, but it had gotten lost in all the wonderfulness. Before he could say another word, Ms. Chalice grabbed him by the hand and dragged him to the midway.

He couldn't believe his eyes.

The midway was the heart of the carnival, the section with all the best rides, games, and cuisine-on-a-stick. In every direction, Cuphead saw something that looked like the most fun he'd ever had in his entire life—well, every direction but one.

"There she is," Ms. Chalice beamed. "Ain't she a beaut?"

Cuphead turned and looked up. And up. And up. From what he could tell, the Dizzy Borden was a twisting, looping torture device created by maniacs who hoped to bring a little more misery into the world. The sight of it made his stomach do somersaults.

"You want to go on that?" he asked.

A lump as big as an acorn jutted out of his throat.

"Well, sure," Ms. Chalice said. "Look at it. It's the bee's knees. The ant's pants. The elephant's adenoids! See how high it climbs? We'll be able to see the whole park from up there! Pretty great way to find Mugman, don't you think?"

Just then, Cuphead heard a ferocious roar and terrified screams. When he turned around, he got his first up-close look at the Dizzy Borden in action. It appeared to be some kind of prison train made up of little carts, where you were strapped in and flung back and forth and upside down at speeds that would peel off your face. None of this sounded helpful.

"Well...," he said.

"What's the matter, Cuphead? You're not scared, are you?"

Scared? How dare she ask if he was scared! Cuphead crossed his arms and scrunched his face into a look of defiance. He'd never been so insulted.

"Of that? Heck no," he lied. "I've seen baby buggies that moved faster."

"Then what's the problem?"

"Oh, there's no problem. It's just that—" He stalled, trying to come up with an excuse. "Well, the track keeps flipping upside down. And if we're upside down, we'll, uh, only see people's feet. You don't expect us to recognize Mugman by his feet, do you?"

Ms. Chalice thought this over. It didn't sound quite right, but it made sense in a Cuphead kind of way. She tried to hide her disappointment—but not very hard.

"I guess not," she muttered. "Oh well, it was just an idea."

"And a dilly of an idea," Cuphead assured her. "We just need a different ride. Like that one."

He pointed to a big, very slow-moving wheel with nice, safe chairs. It looked a lot like sitting on a park bench, but without the thrills.

"The Ferris wheel?" Ms. Chalice groaned.

"Sure! Look how high it goes. It's the perfect ride for looking around."

Ms. Chalice rolled her eyes. Now she'd be stuck on a dull ol' Ferris wheel and never get to ride the roller coaster. But if they wanted to find Mugman, she supposed it would do.

Cuphead gave a sigh of relief. He'd managed to avoid the Dizzy Borden and still keep his reputation as the most courageous boy on the Inkwell Isles. As far as he was concerned, things couldn't have worked out better.

"Two, please," he told the Ferris wheel operator, and reached into his pocket.

That was strange. It felt a lot emptier than it had earlier. But he figured with all the running they were doing, the money was bound to have settled a little.

He was about to dig deeper (it was sure to be in there somewhere) when the ride runner cleared his throat the way rude people do when they're tired of waiting. So he reached into his other pocket (Cuphead always kept a few things in his other pocket so he wouldn't walk lopsided) and pulled out a couple of nickels. The next thing he knew, they were on the Ferris wheel, climbing high into the air.

"Just look at this view," he said, smiling. "Isn't it swell?"

"Whoopee," grumbled Ms. Chalice. "Wait'll I tell the kids at school."

She didn't sound very sincere, but it didn't matter since Cuphead wasn't listening. There was too much to see. As they reached the top of the wheel, he realized he could look out over the whole carnival. It really was a sensation. He saw the Stilt-a-whirl (where you were spun around by a man on stilts), the Hat-a-pult (which catapulted you out of an enormous derby), the Yak-robats (possibly the bendiest yaks ever to put on leotards), and lots of other rides and shows and attractions—and something else.

"Eureka!" he yelled.

Ms. Chalice got very excited.

"You found Mugman!" she cheered.

But Cuphead hadn't found Mugman. He had, however, found the next best thing.

"It's Cala Maria," he said. "I'd know her anywhere."

Sure enough, the isles' best-known mermaid was standing at the other end of the midway having a delicious-looking frozen vanilla phosphate on a stick. Cuphead didn't see Mugman, but there was a good chance he'd be nearby.

"Now all we have to do is get down from here," he said.

Only... that wouldn't be as easy as it sounded.

You see, the Ferris wheel operator who normally got riders up into the air and back down again was not at his usual post. Instead, there were three replacements: Beppi the Clown, Sally Stageplay, and Djimmi the Great.

"Are those the ones?" asked Beppi.

"That's them. They're the brats who ruined my show," said Sally.

"Show?" snapped Djimmi. "They nearly got me killed!"

Typical villains, always blaming someone else for their problems. It's true their encounters with

Cuphead and Ms. Chalice hadn't gone very well. Sally was a patchwork of bandages, Djimmi's arm was in a sling, and Beppi wore an ice pack like a little French hat. Still, only a monster would try to take revenge on two helpless children.

Which, of course, is exactly what they did.

Beppi (who, as a clown, understood that timing is everything) waited until Cuphead's chair reached the very top of the Ferris wheel before he calmly extended his hand and pulled a long, rusty lever. The ride stopped.

"Hey!" yelled Cuphead. "What's the big idea?"

You couldn't blame him for being annoyed. Just when it looked like they might actually track down Mugman, they ended up stuck on a gigantic wheel of misfortune.

"Get us moving, will you?" he groaned.

And in the gravity-deprived seconds that followed, he groaned even more. But then, like ice cracking on a frozen pond, that terrible, twisted smile returned to Beppi's face.

"You heard the boy," he told Djimmi. "Get 'em moving."

Nothing could have pleased the genie more. He

stood next to the Ferris wheel and said these words: "One for the money, two for the show, three to get ready, now watch me grow!"

And grow he did. He grew until he was every bit as tall as the ride, and maybe an inch or two taller. Grabbing hold of the spokes, he gave the wheel a good hard spin.

It whirled like the blades on an electric fan.

Cuphead screamed. His stomach was where his eyeballs should be, his eyeballs were where his brain should be, and his brain floated above him like a squishy little cloud. He grabbed the chair and held on for dear life, wondering how he'd ever make this up to Ms. Chalice.

"*Wheeeeeeeeeeeeeeeee!*" she squealed. "Now, this is more like it!"

Sally, who never appreciated any performance that wasn't her own, had seen enough. She raised her parasol and poked the giant genie in the ankle.

"She's enjoying it, you magical meathead! Do something!"

Djimmi took a deep breath, the kind that made his eyes bulge and his chest puff out like a vacuum cleaner bag, and blew. It hit the ride with the force of a hurricane, whirling the wheel so fast you could barely see it. This time, there was no scream from Cuphead, and no squeal from Ms. Chalice—there was only the sight of them being flung out of their seat and sent streaking across the sky.

Now, if you've never been thrown from a Ferris wheel and sent sailing halfway across a carnival, you probably think the worst place you could land would be on top of a bear. But you would be wrong. The worst place would be on top of a bear riding a unicycle across a tightrope during an aerial act, which Cuphead discovered completely by accident. On the bright side, the audience seemed to enjoy this new twist on an old standard, and they burst into wild applause. They grew even louder when, a moment later, Ms. Chalice landed on Cuphead's shoulders, forming the rarely seen girl-boy-bear triple-decker sandwich on a unicycle.

"Sorry to drop in on you," she apologized.

But the balancing bear had bigger problems. With Ms. Chalice's arrival, the tightrope stretched downward, then sprung back up like an archer's bowstring, sending the little one-wheeled contraption flying into the crowd. Carnival-goers leaped out of the way as the teetering trio blazed down the midway.

They might have rolled right out the front gate and on to parts unknown had they not first run into the strongman, who was lifting a heavy-looking dumbbell, and then into an unfortunately placed cotton-candy cart. Even so, they continued for a good distance, but a pink, gooey ball of fluff containing a bear, two hitchhikers, and a strongman can roll only so far, and they crashed—with a *splat* and a *thud* and an *oof*—into the aisle.

When Cuphead looked up, he saw a pair of sparkling eyes staring down at him. It was Cala Maria.

13

JUST PLANE HUMILIATIN'

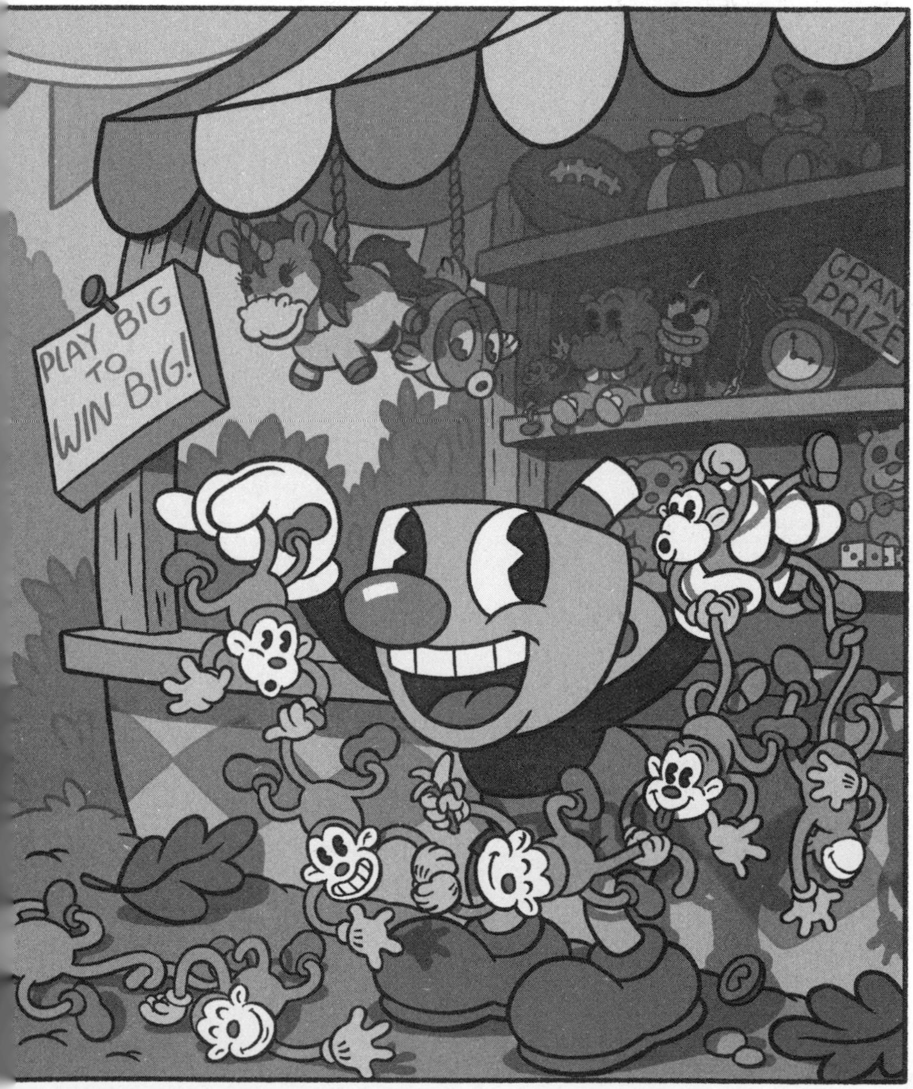
PLAY BIG TO WIN BIG!

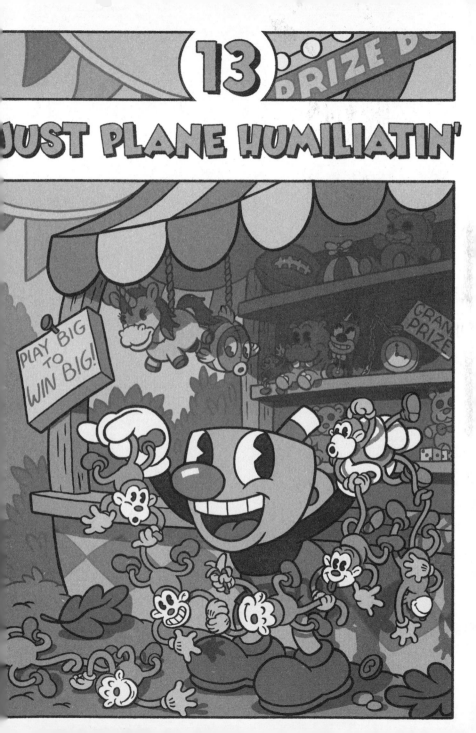

A ll right, where's Mugman?" Cuphead demanded.
Cala Maria gave a bored sigh. "Same place
he's been the past half hour."

She pointed into the air.

Cuphead looked up. There was Mugman, riding
in a tiny airplane twirling round and round on a
chain. He wore a smile that, if anything, was bigger
than his face.

"The kiddie planes?"

"He won't get off," Cala Maria said.

It was true. At first, Mugman had been completely
under her power. He'd bought her candied crabapples,
corny crunchies, butter kabobs, beans-on-a-biscuit,
pickle sickles, and lots of other tomfoodery. But all
that changed when he spotted the airplane ride.

"It was like . . . I didn't even exist anymore," she
said.

Cuphead understood completely. Mugman had always been crazy about flying (he'd once spent a week in a nest of baby birds, hoping the family would adopt him). But this was taking it too far. It was bad enough he'd come to the carnival, but to end up spinning around on a ride meant for babies—well, that was just embarrassing.

"Mugman!" he called out.

Mugman looked down from the tiny aircraft.

"Oh! Hi, Cuphead!" he sang. "Look at me! Look at me! I'm flying!"

Cuphead rolled his eyes.

"You come down from there right now!"

Ms. Chalice, who had been pulling the last of the cotton candy from underneath her armpits, joined Cuphead and Cala Maria beside the ride. She shook her head.

"Airplanes," she said. "We should've known."

At last, the ride twirled slower and slower until the planes hung down like pom-poms on a lampshade. Mugman crawled out of the cockpit.

"Hello, Ms. Chalice. Have you met Cala Maria?" he asked. "We've been seeing the carnival."

Seeing the carnival? *Seeing the carnival?* Cuphead's

face turned pink, then red, then purplish mulberry. Finally, a burst of steam blew out of his straw.

"You're unbelievable!" he snapped. "Do you realize we've been looking everywhere for you? We've only got an hour until Elder Kettle's birthday party, we still don't have a present, and here you were spending good money on kiddie rides!"

"Oh, not just on rides Cuphead," said Mugman. "Cala Maria won me this."

He held up a small tin monkey—the worst prize in the entire carnival. It looked like something that might come out of a gumball machine if you weren't lucky enough to get something more valuable, such as a gumball.

"I told him I'd win him a stuffed animal, but he wanted that instead," said Cala Maria.

Ms. Chalice looked confused.

"What are you going to do with a tin monkey?" she asked.

"Put it with these," said Mugman, and he held up a long chain of little tin monkeys linked by their arms. "Look, they're holding hands."

He couldn't have been more pleased. Cala Maria had seen enough.

"Well, it's been fun, but I have to be going now," she said. "Oh, I almost forgot. You said if I won you the monkey, you'd buy me a souvenir postcard, remember?"

She pressed Mugman's nose with her finger. His eyes immediately flashed the word *sale*, a bell rang like on a cash register, and his tongue popped out like a drawer. There was a dollar on it.

"Thanks, flyboy," Cala Maria said, and she took the bill and strolled happily down the midway.

"Well, if that don't beat all," said Cuphead. "How much money do you have left, anyway?"

Mugman checked.

"None," he said. "But I'm rich in monkeys."

Feeling suddenly nervous, Ms. Chalice reached into her pocket. It was empty.

"Uh-oh," she said. "I've been burgled."

Now it was Cuphead's turn. He reached back into the pocket that had seemed suspiciously light during his encounter with the Ferris wheel operator. This time, he dug deep—all the way to the bottom, and through the hole, and through the hole in the hole. But when his fingers arrived in Pocket Town, all they found were little lint tumbleweeds blowing down the street.

Cuphead's stomach twisted into a knot. He checked his other pocket. There were two marbles, a paper clip, a fuzzy lemon-drop, and twenty-five cents.

This was a disaster.

"Oh well, at least we still have our health," said Mugman, and that was true.

But whether they could keep it was an entirely different matter.

14

BRINEYBEARD TO THE RESCUE

Cuphead, Mugman, and Ms. Chalice took a slow, sad walk down the midway. Elder Kettle was right. The carnival was filled with liars and thieves, and they were wrong to have ever come here. The three of them were hungry and tired, and their money was gone, but worse than all that was the constant, agonizing feeling of guilt. Everyone was counting on them to bring Elder Kettle a wonderful birthday present, and what did they have for him?

Nothing.

They collapsed into a miserable heap in front of a short wooden fence.

"What kind of present can we buy with a lousy twenty-five cents?" Cuphead groaned.

Mugman and Ms. Chalice weren't listening. But that didn't mean he wasn't heard.

"Avast, ye matey," came a gruff, booming voice from

above. "Sounds like you're drownin' in a sea of troubles. But worry not, lad—ol' Brineybeard's here to rescue you!"

When Cuphead looked up, he saw an upside-down face staring back at him. It had an eye patch and a thick black beard and a grin as wide as a mainsail.

"Rescue?" he asked.

Cuphead climbed to his feet and discovered the fence they were leaning against wasn't a fence at all—it was the front of a carnival booth. The bearded man was leaning through a window above them.

"Captain Brineybeard, at your service," he said. "I couldn't help overhearin' you've a need for a gift."

"It's a birthday present for Elder Kettle," Mugman told him.

"*Arr*, it's a fine thing to honor a man on his birthday," Brineybeard said. "And as it happens, I have a hull full of treasures right here, each of them available for only, say . . . twenty-five cents?"

"Only twenty-five cents?" Cuphead said excitedly.

"Aye. That is, if you can win them."

The captain smiled. It was the kind of happy, salty smile that could come only from someone who knows just the right time to sing a sea chantey. This was not that time. (The truth is, now that he'd become a landlubber, Brineybeard was interested in only one kind of ship—salesmanship.) He held out a ball.

"Care to try your luck?" he asked.

Cuphead stared at the perfect little sphere. It was round and white with horseshoe-shaped stitching, just like the ball Hilda Berg had returned that morning. He reached for it—and felt himself yanked backward by his collar.

"My brother doesn't have any luck," Mugman said, pulling Cuphead away from the booth. "He's all out."

It was true. If Cuphead had learned nothing else today, he'd learned luck didn't last very long at the carnival.

"Sorry, Captain," he told Brineybeard. "Save it for the rubes."

Brineybeard frowned and rubbed his furry chin. He leaned an elbow on the counter.

"Oh well, you can't blame an ol' salt for tryin'. I just thought with you needin' a present, and this bein' the easiest game on the whole midway, then—"

"Easiest?" said Cuphead.

He pulled away from Mugman. The captain smiled again.

"Aye, that it be," he said. "This game ain't nothin' to a boy who knows how to pitch. Why, it'd be like throwin' at a sittin' duck."

"And what exactly would I be throwing at? I don't see any targets." Cuphead asked.

Instantly, the front of the booth popped open, displaying a big sign that said DUNK-A-QUACK.

"Sittin' ducks," Brineybeard said proudly.

Cautiously, Cuphead peeked over the counter. Sure enough, there were five ducks sitting on five little ledges. They didn't look particularly cunning. Or quick. Or even interested. One was taking a nap, one was reading a newspaper, the third was wearing a black derby hat and smoking a cigar, and the last two were playing a game of canasta. It really did look easy.

"Look, mate, all you gotta do is hit the target and the duck falls into the water tank. It's a piece-a-cake. Whadda'ya say?"

Cuphead thought it over. He knew he shouldn't spend their last twenty-five cents on a carnival game, but this was pitching—the thing he was born to do! He looked at Ms. Chalice. She shook her head.

"No dice, Brineybeard," he said.

The three of them were just about to leave (which is exactly what Elder Kettle would've wanted them to do), when the duck with the black derby hat and cigar stood up on his ledge.

"So you're just gonna walk away, eh?" he said. "What's a matter, kid? Chicken?"

Well, if you know anything at all about ducks and chickens, you know they don't get along very well, and never will. So of all the names a duck might call someone (and keep in mind they practically invented fowl language), "chicken" is by far the most insulting.

No one understood this better than Cuphead. He clenched his fists and stuck out his chin.

"What'd you say?" he growled, taking a step toward the booth.

Ms. Chalice moved in front of him.

"Take it easy, Cuphead. He's just trying to get to you," she said.

Cuphead stared at the duck and frowned.

"Phooey," he said, spitting on the ground. "We're gettin' outta here."

"Aw, let him go," the other card-playing duck shouted. "He's probably got a rag arm, anyway."

Cuphead gritted his teeth.

"You're right, who needs him?" said the derby-wearing duck. "Hey fellas, let's say goodbye in a way he can understand."

All the ducks leaped from their seats.

"BOK! Bok bok BOK! Bok BOK!" they clucked, then laughed so hard they nearly fell off their ledges.

"Just ignore them, Cuphead," Mugman said.

Cuphead tried. But his steps were becoming increasingly stompy.

"All right, matey, have it your way," Brineybeard called out. "But I sure hate for you to miss out on these fabulous prizes. Dunk just one duck, and you get a genuine tin monkey."

Mugman turned around, but Ms. Chalice stopped him.

"You're wasting your breath," Cuphead yelled back.

"Two ducks gets you a whistle. Three, a comb. Four, a stuffed bear, and if you get all five—"

"I won't, because I'm not playing."

"If you get all five," he continued, "you get a gold pocket watch and chain."

Cuphead froze in his tracks. He could not have

moved his legs if he wanted to. Instead, his head spun all the way around until it faced Brineybeard.

"Did you say pocket watch?"

"And chain," the captain said. "And all you have to do is dunk some sittin' ducks."

It did look easy. Too easy.

"Well, I don't know...."

Brineybeard's face broke into the widest grin yet.

"I'll tell you what I'm gonna do. Just to show you how simple it is, I'll let you take the first throw for free."

15

CUPHEAD DUNKS A DUCK

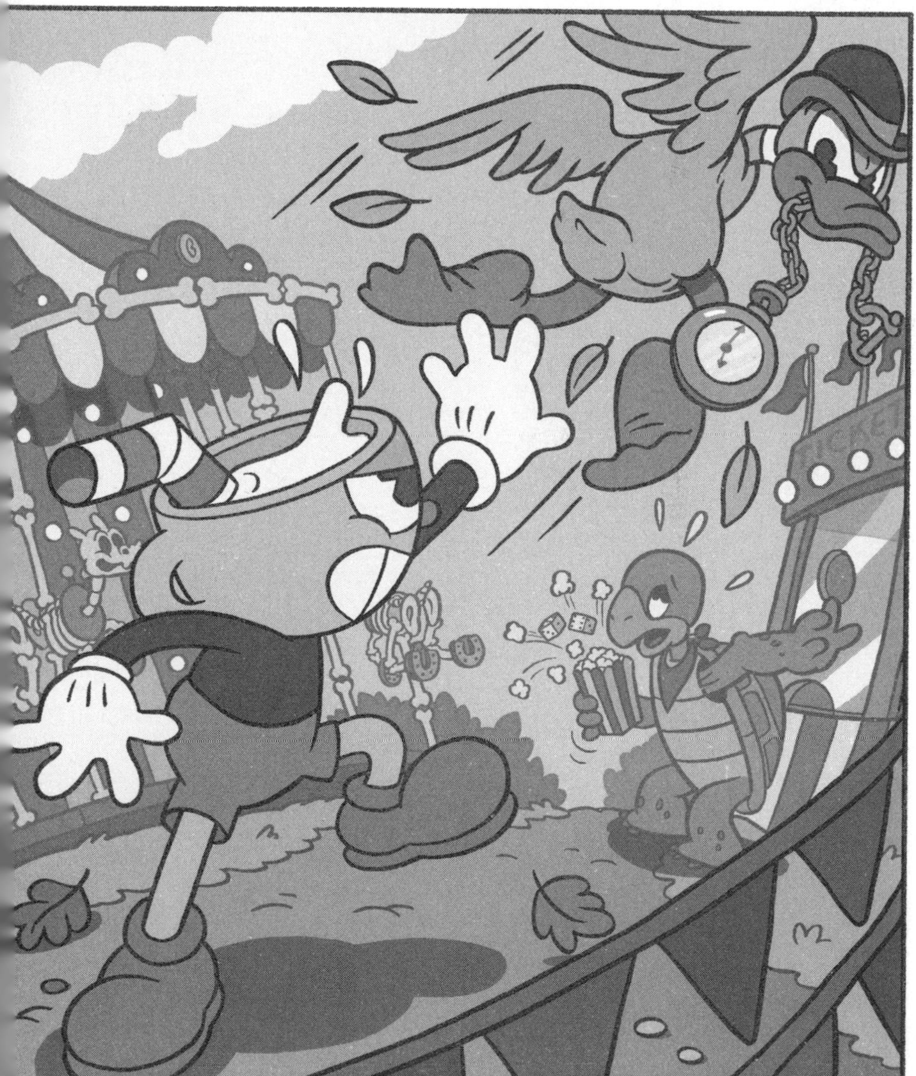

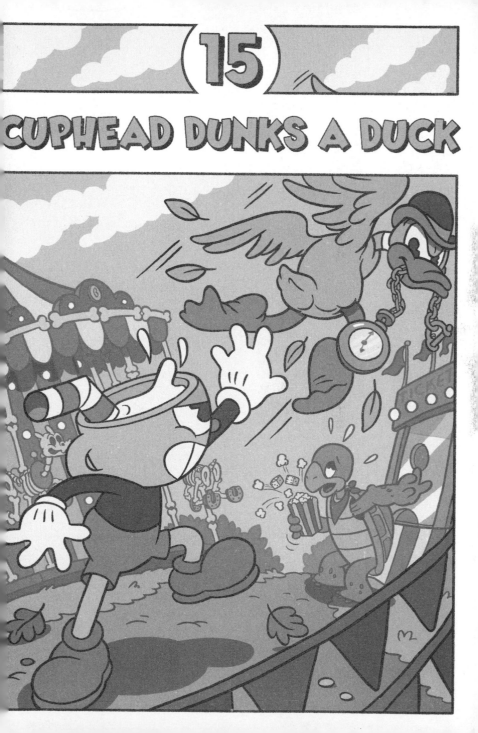

Free? At the carnival? It sounded too good to be true. Still, Cuphead wasn't sure he could trust a pirate—they were a terrible nuisance on the water, and he couldn't imagine them being much better on land. And he definitely didn't care for those ducks. He looked at Mugman and Ms. Chalice.

"What have we got to lose?" Ms. Chalice shrugged.

Good ol' Ms. Chalice. She had a real knack for getting to the nittiest part of the gritty. So, as a group, the three of them made a quick, looping U-turn and headed back to the booth.

"Can I see the watch first?" Cuphead asked.

Brineybeard smiled and lifted his hand from behind the counter. A beautiful gold pocket watch dangled from his fingers. It was even nicer than the one in Porkrind's store.

"Okay, I'll take a throw," Cuphead told him.

Brineybeard handed him the ball. He rubbed the cool white horsehide against his palm.

"Well, look who's back," said the derbied duck. "If it ain't my ol' pal, chicken-boy. What's that you got in your hand there, chicken-boy? Don't tell me you laid an egg!"

The bigmouthed birds were in stitches. They cackled and clucked, and Cuphead felt his face turning the color of tomato soup. Meanwhile, his chief tormentor tugged down his hat and braced himself for the pitch.

"So, you think you can dunk me, do you? Well, take your best shot!"

Instantly, the dugout ducks broke into ballgame chatter. They said things like "Atta boy, atta boy, put it in there, pal!" and "Right down the ol' pike, you got 'em, sport!" and "No meatballs, ace, just toss 'em a yakker and put some mustard on it!"

They were so loud and so enthusiastic that if Cuphead hadn't known better, he'd have sworn they were rooting for him. The truth is, with Mugman and Ms. Chalice looking on, the whole thing felt almost like a real ballgame. He pictured himself in a stadium in front of a crowd of cheering fans.

Now pitching for the Inkwell Inkspots, said an imaginary announcer, *Cuphead!*

"Go on, Cuphead," Mugman told him. "You can do it."

Cuphead snapped out of his daydream. Sitting across from him were the five ducks, each of them looking as smug as ever. He picked a target, stared at the big red bull's-eye, and went into his windup. Then, like a cannon firing a mighty shot, he rocketed the ball across the booth. It soared through open space, made an impressive dipsy-doodle, and then—

CLANGGGGGGG!

It nailed the target. The ledge opened like a trapdoor, and the foulest of the fowl plummeted into the tank, leaving behind a derby and a floating cigar.

"Help! Help!" he cried, splashing frantically in the water. "I can't swim! I can't swim!"

"But you're a duck," Mugman reminded him.

"Oh yeah," said the duck, who immediately stopped drowning and started doing the backstroke. "Look at me, I'm waterproof!"

Of course, his feathered friends thought this was hysterical. They fell on their backs and grabbed their stomachs and kicked their feet up and down before finally helping the wise-quacker back onto the ledge.

"So, what do you say, lad?" Brineybeard asked. "Are you ready to win that watch?"

Cuphead wanted to win the watch, and he really wanted to dunk another duck. Still, it was their last quarter. For a dilemma as big as this, he needed advice (preferably in the form of a musical number, which was the style at the time).

So it was a good thing the Four Mel Arrangement just happened to be passing by.

We hear you're quite a PITCHER, *we hear you've got an*
   ARM—
(Bom, bom, bom)
We hear your blazing fastball once set off a fire ALARM—
(Bom, bom, bom)
Now all of us are hoping you take home that watch and
   chainnnnnnnnnnnn—
(Bom, bom, bom, BOM *)*
So DUNK *those* DUCKS *and send your* BIRTHDAY
   worries down the DRAIN*!*

As soon as the song was over, the little quartet disappeared. And so did Cuphead's doubts about what he had to do.

"You heard the Mels," he said. "Give me the ball."

The more he thought about it, the more Cuphead was convinced this was the right decision, and not just because it had come to him in four-part harmony. After all, how else were they going to get Elder Kettle a nice watch? Or anything else, for that matter? And if, in the process, he happened to settle the hash of a bunch of bad-mannered mallards, where was the harm in that? No, after giving it careful consideration, he was absolutely sure this was the smartest thing he'd ever done, and that was all there was to it.

As for why Ms. Chalice was frowning, he had no idea.

"*Psssst,*" she said, motioning for him to come closer.

Cuphead waved her away. "I can do this."

"Sure, you could, if it was fair," she whispered. "But I've got a sneaky feeling this game is crooked."

Just then, the booth rocked crookedly to one side until it looked like a sinking ship sticking out of the water. Brineybeard quickly picked up the slumping edge and stuck a rock under it, making the whole thing as straight as the innocent-looking grin on his face.

Ms. Chalice crossed her arms.

"It's just a coincidence," Cuphead told her, and he handed the captain their last quarter.

He took the ball, rolled it between his fingers, and gave the ducks a steely-eyed stare (steely-eyed being the unfriendliest of all the sports stares). But oddly enough, the ducks didn't stare back. They didn't mock him or taunt him or egg him on with contagious ballpark banter. In fact, they seemed completely uninterested. They'd gone back to playing cards or reading the newspaper or smoking cigars or napping just as they had been when he'd arrived. Hard as it was to believe, this absolute indifference was even more distracting than their shenanigans. Cuphead put it out of his mind and focused on the targets. Each one had a red bull's-eye as big as a pomegranate—a good pitcher couldn't miss. This was a cinch.

He went through his elaborate, multistep windup and drilled the ball at the first target. The pitch could not have been truer, and just when it looked like a direct hit—

THUD!

One of the ducks—the one behind the newspaper— stuck a catcher's mitt in front of it.

"That's not fair! He used a catcher's mitt!" Ms. Chalice complained.

"A catcher's mitt? I don't see no catcher's mitt," lied Brineybeard.

The ducks all whistled innocently.

"Next pitch!" The pirate grinned and handed Cuphead another ball.

Cuphead narrowed his eyes and bit his lip. He'd just have to try harder, that's all. This time, he twisted his arm until it wound up like a rubber band, then launched his screwball. It whipped, and whirled, and headed straight for the bull's-eye, and then—

TWEEEEEEEEET!

The napping duck blew a whistle. And since he was now wearing a traffic cop's uniform and holding up a small stop sign, the ball screeched to a halt. A second later, the target swung upward like a crossing gate, the red bull's-eye turned green, and—*WHOOSH!*—the ball sped harmlessly underneath it.

"Hey, you said these were sitting ducks!" Cuphead complained.

"Aye, they be sittin'," Brineybeard said. "Why, them's the sittin'est ducks I ever did see."

Cuphead sighed. How had he convinced himself this game would be fair? It was a carnival, and carnivals were filled with liars and thieves, just like Elder Kettle said. All he could do now was take his lumps. He threw the third pitch (which was batted back with a tennis racket), and the fourth (which was incinerated by a flamethrower), and solemnly held out his hand.

Brineybeard passed him the fifth and final ball.

"Don't worry, Cuphead," Ms. Chalice said. "You'll get this one."

"Big deal," Cuphead grumbled. "It's the last ball. What are we supposed to do—give Elder Kettle a tin monkey?"

"If he doesn't want it, I know someone who does!" Mugman beamed.

Cuphead rolled his eyes and, out of habit, went into the long windup for his pitch. He was just about to make the painfully pointless throw when Ms. Chalice screamed, "Wait!"

Cuphead froze like a statue in mid-toss.

"I've got an idea," she said. "Mel, Melvin, Melroy, and Melbert—come with me."

The Four Mels popped up from behind the counter and followed Ms. Chalice to the center of the midway. It was very crowded.

"Attention, everybody!" she yelled. "How about a sing-along?"

Well, if you've ever been to the Inkwell Isles, you know how they feel about their sing-alongs. No sooner had the words left her mouth than a huge group of communal crooners came running from all directions.

"Everybody ready?" she shouted.

"But I don't know the words," yelled a stranger.

"Oh, don't worry about that," she told him. "Just follow the bouncing ball!"

Ah, the bouncing ball—where would sing-alongs be without it? As you know, whenever synchronized songsters come together, lyrics appear overhead as if on some invisible magic movie screen. Then a big red ball arrives from out of nowhere and bounces from word to word to help everyone sing along. So it was no surprise at all when that very thing happened as Mel,

Mel, Mel, and Mel led the crowd in a merry melody that went like this:

> We're SINGIN' a SWINGIN' song—
> (BOM, bom, BOM, bom)
> SO come JOIN us and SING along—
> (BOM, bom, BOM, bom)
> Don't KNOW the WORDS?
> No TROUBLE at ALL—
> Just FOLLOW the BOUNCING ball!

When the red ball struck the last note, it bounced right off the end of the lyric sheet and right into Ms. Chalice's hands. She turned it over and peeked at the underside, which read:

MANUFACTURED BY
ACME SING-A-LONG COMPANY
"A THOUSAND BOUNCES IN EVERY BALL!"

It was just what she needed. She rushed back to the booth, where Cuphead was still frozen in his pitching pose.

"Sorry for the holdup," she said, and put the bouncing ball into his outstretched hand. "Okay, go ahead."

Cuphead threw the red ball as hard as he could. Only this time, he missed the target completely (an embarrassing blunder for anyone who called himself a pitcher), and the ducks laughed and laughed and—

BOINNNNNNNNNNG.

The rubber ball hit the back of the booth and bounced . . . and bounced . . . and bounced. It ricocheted off the first target, dunking the duck with the newspaper. Then it hit the second target, dunking the sleeping duck. It dunked one of the card-playing ducks, then sprung back and drenched his partner. Before Cuphead knew what was happening, four ducks were splashing around in the tank, and only one was left on his ledge. . . . Derby duck.

But even though the ball was zipping and zinging around the booth at supersonic speed, the smug, smirking bird just sat there smirking smugly. He didn't flinch an inch. Finally, the peppy projectile made a beeline straight for him. Impact was imminent. A soaking was certain. But just as he was about to take one right in the kisser, he ducked (which, of course, is what ducks do) and the ball sailed past him.

"Ha-ha! You missed me!" he squealed, blowing a raspberry with his tongue. "Why, you couldn't hit a—"

BOINNNNNNNNNG!

Poor duck. It seemed he'd forgotten one thing about rubber balls: They don't just bounce, they bounce back. The wily whizzer ricocheted off the rear wall, goosed him in the tail feathers, and sent him into a swan dive.

"No fair!" Brineybeard bellowed. "That's cheatin', that's a hornswoggle, that's—"

BONNNNNNK!

His speech came to a sudden and unexpected stop. You see, it turned out the ball had used only 999 of its thousand bounces, meaning there was still one left for the captain. He joined his crew in the tank.

"That's five dunked ducks and one soggy sea captain!" cheered Ms. Chalice. "Cuphead wins!"

"I'll take the watch, please," Cuphead said.

Brineybeard spit out a mouthful of water, climbed out of the tank, and made a sad, squishy walk to the prize case. In all the time he'd been operating the booth, he'd never had to give a prize away. Not one. This was a shameful day for carnival pirates. He grabbed the watch and held it out like a smelly sock he'd picked up off the floor.

Cuphead took it.

"Just a second," the duck with the dripping derby howled. He crossed the booth and stood in front of Cuphead. "I never thought you could do it, kid. But you beat us fair and square. Just to show there's no hard feelings, I'd like to shake your hand."

He extended a wing, and Cuphead (who, win or lose, was always a good sport) held out his hand. When he did, the feathered felon quickly snatched the watch, flapped his wings, and flew out of the booth.

"So long, suckers," he laughed.

Cuphead couldn't believe it. He just stood there, staring at his empty hand. The watch was gone. Gone! He wheeled around and pointed to the skedaddling scoundrel.

"Follow that duck!"

16

HAREBRAINED SCHEMES

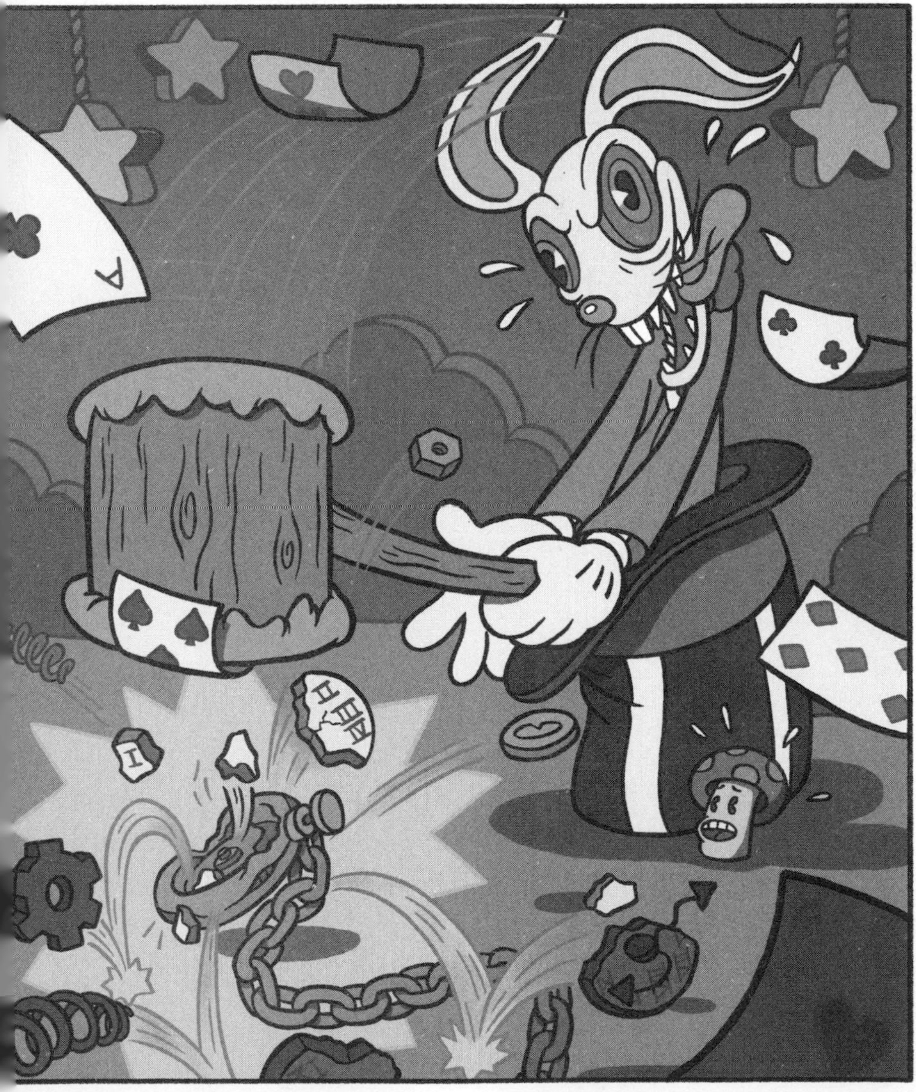

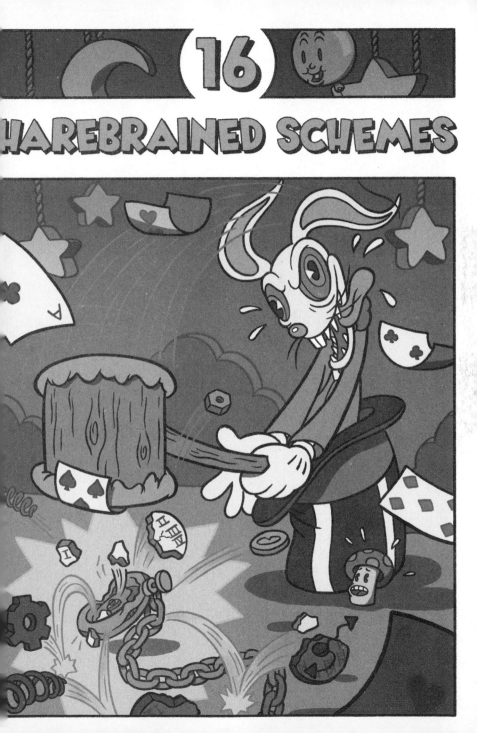

It was a depressing turn of events. The dastardly duck had stolen not just a watch, but any hope of giving Elder Kettle a happy birthday. As the thief soared above the carnival crowd, Cuphead, Mugman, and Ms. Chalice chased after him on foot.

"Excuse me, coming through, sorry," Cuphead said as they raced down the midway.

"There he is! Over there!" yelled Ms. Chalice.

She was right, of course. (Ms. Chalice was an avid birdwatcher and had a surprisingly good eye for hats.) The duck had landed at the far end of the aisle and was now running. The three friends were in hot pursuit when suddenly, the bird veered off the path and bolted inside one of the large tents lining the midway. This was their chance.

Like knights storming a castle, the unstoppable trio dashed into the tent—and stopped. They had to. It turned out this was a show tent, one packed so tightly the audience had to take turns breathing. But the most unusual thing about this group wasn't its size, it was that it was made up entirely of ducks.

Cuphead looked around. There were ducks to the left of them, ducks to the right, here a duck, there a duck, everywhere a duck duck. It would have been laughable if it weren't so tragic.

"How are we going to find a duck in here?" he groaned.

"Easy," said a duck standing next to him. "Just use a duck call!"

"Quack, quack, quack, quack!" the crowd laughed. (You hear a lot of bad things about ducks, but they appreciate a good joke.)

There was something curious about these fowl festivities. Cuphead couldn't help noticing that almost everyone was wearing a fez. And if there's one thing more unusual than a room full of ducks, it's a room full of ducks wearing bright-red matching hats.

"What's going on here?" he asked.

"Why, the convention, of course. We're the International Order of Odd Ducks, Flock 158," said the duck. "Say, you're not a member."

"Yes, I know," said Cuphead.

"So, what are you doing here?"

"We're looking for someone," Cuphead said.

"A duck?" asked the duck.

Cuphead nodded.

"So I guess that makes you," the duck said, and paused for effect, "A DUCK HUNTER!"

"Quack, quack, quack, quack!" Flock 158 screamed.

Well, as much as Cuphead would've liked to stand around chatting with a bunch of joke-telling, fez-wearing waterfowl (and who knew when he'd have the chance again?), he had to find Elder Kettle's watch before the party. He was running out of time.

"I'm going to look over there," he said, and pushed his way into the friendly, fezzy flock.

But just as he was edging toward the front of the crowd, everything went black. In a flash, a blindingly bright spotlight lit up the stage. The show was starting.

"Greetings, fellow Odd Ducks," announced a plump mallard wearing a novelty fez with an arrow through it. "We have a heckuva show for you tonight. By special order of the Grand Quacker himself, I present to you the amazing, the astounding Hopus Pocus!"

The ducks clapped and whistled and quacked, and then got tired and stopped because absolutely nothing was happening. Cuphead looked at the stage. It was empty. If this Hopus Pocus had hoped to make an entrance, he'd missed his cue. In fact, the only sign anything at all was going on was a quiet, rhythmic thumping sound coming from offstage.

Thump . . . thump . . . thump.

There it was again. He wondered what it could be. A moment later, an upside-down black-felt top hat hopped across the stage and into the spotlight.

"For my first trick," the top hat said, "I will pull a rabbit out of a hat."

Cuphead was confused. Where was the magician? This trick seemed to be missing one of its most important pieces. But then a white glove stuck straight up out of the hat. It was attached to a long blue sleeve that appeared to be some kind of well-dressed arm. Then, in a very theatrical manner, the glove reached into the hat, and when it emerged again, it pulled out a pair of long white ears and a fluffy white head and finally, an entire rabbit.

"Ta-da!" the rabbit said.

The ducks cheered. They'd seen a magician pull

a rabbit out of a hat before, but never quite like this.

Hopus Pocus might have been a rabbit, but he fit right in with the International Order of Odd Ducks because he was, well, odd. He wore a blue tuxedo and red bow tie that accentuated his deranged expression and bulging yellow eyes. But the strangest thing about him was his behavior. It was almost as if he were half magician, half monster—and you were never really sure which half you were watching.

"For my next trick," he said, "I'll need a volunteer"— a hundred wings shot into the air—"who isn't a duck."

The wings came back down.

"How about you?" he said.

"Me?" asked Cuphead.

"Why not? You're not a duck, are you?"

"No," said Cuphead.

The rabbit raised an eyebrow.

"And you're not a chicken?"

"Quack, quack, quack, quack, quack!" laughed the Odd Ducks.

Cuphead frowned.

"No," he said, gruffer this time.

"Then what are you waiting for?" the rabbit asked.

Suddenly, Cuphead was lifted into the air and passed from duck to duck until he reached the stage. Hopus gave him a wicked grin.

"What's your name, kid?"

"Cuphead. I'm here with my friends Mugman and Ms. Chalice, and we're looking for—"

"Great, fascinating, glad to hear it," the rabbit told him. "Now get in the box."

Cuphead turned around. There was a long wooden box on the stage. When he crawled inside, his head stuck out one end, his feet out the other.

"Will you look at that? A perfect fit," said Hopus. "Let me ask you something, kid: Are you really attached to those legs?"

Cuphead gulped. "Uh-huh."

"Well," said Hopus, breaking into a smile. "We'll take care of that!"

With fantastic speed, he whipped out a large, spinning buzz saw.

"Cuphead!" Mugman yelled, but there was nothing he could do.

"And now, my fine feathered friends," Hopus proclaimed, "I will saw my volunteer in half!"

And one quick buzz later, he'd done just that.

At first, Cuphead was too stunned to do anything. Then he wiggled his toes, just to make sure they still worked. They did—which was strange, since they were on the other side of the stage.

"Hey, what's the big idea?" he yelled.

"Take it easy, pal," Hopus told him. "Pull yourself together!"

The audience quacked hysterically.

Cuphead gritted his teeth and kicked his feet, and though they were nowhere near each other, you could tell both halves were equally angry.

"I can't stay like this; I've got things to do. Fix me!" he demanded.

Hopus yawned.

"Yeah, yeah, in a minute, kid. First, I got a show to do," he said, and turned back to the audience. "Now, does anyone have a watch?"

To Cuphead's astonishment, a duck with a black derby hat—the very same duck Cuphead had been chasing—climbed up on to the stage. He was smiling.

"As a matter of fact, I do," the duck said, and held out the gold pocket watch.

"That's mine!" yelled Cuphead.

Hopus took the watch.

"My, this is a nice one. A real beauty."

"It was given to me by my poor ol' gran-mudder," said the duck.

Cuphead couldn't stand it any longer. He kicked his feet until the box tipped forward, and when he was upright, the downstairs half of him stomped furiously across the stage.

"It was not given to him by his poor ol' grandmother," his upper half shouted. "He stole it from me!"

Now the ducks booed. Hopus held up his hands.

"Happens every time, folks," he said. "You put a kid in the show and he goes to pieces."

"Quack, quack, quack, quack!" the crowd laughed hysterically.

Hopus strolled over to the talking half of Cuphead.

"If I put you back together, will you get off the stage?"

"Not without my watch," said Cuphead.

"Fine, but you don't get it until I finish my act."

"Fine!" Cuphead shouted.

With that, the magician grabbed hold of the box

with the top half of Cuphead and rolled it into the one with the lower half. The boxes tumbled to the ground, and—like magic—out fell a full-size Cuphead. His feet and face reunited, he marched across the stage and gave the cigar-chomping duck a stare that would curdle cheese.

Meanwhile, Hopus went on with his show.

"About this watch," he said. "Does it have any sentimental value?"

"It is my most cherished possession," the bird lied.

"I see," said the rabbit, and he got a wild look in his eyes. "So I definitely shouldn't do this!"

Without warning, he pulled a large hammer from behind his back, and—*WHACK!*—smashed the watch to bits.

The audience gasped. The derbied duck laughed. Cuphead nearly fainted. The watch that was supposed to be Elder Kettle's birthday present was destroyed!

"Oops, clumsy me," Hopus apologized. "Oh well, let me just sweep that up."

He took out a small whisk broom and swept the pieces into his hat.

After a lot of pushing and shoving, Mugman and

Ms. Chalice finally made their way to the stage. They rushed over to Cuphead, but he pulled away from them and set his eyes on Hopus.

"What kind of magician are you?" he snapped. "You busted my watch!"

"Oh, did I?" the rabbit said, and reached into the hat.

When he pulled out the watch, it was completely repaired. The crowd went wild, as did Cuphead, who'd never been more relieved in his life.

"Thank goodness," he said. "Jeepers, did you save us from a disaster! Now if I can just have the watch . . ."

"Not so fast," Hopus reminded him. "I said not until I finished my act, remember? And I've got one last trick."

The rabbit grinned, dangled the watch in front of him, and jumped into the hat.

Cuphead rushed over and looked inside. The hat was empty. Appallingly, depressingly, heartbreakingly empty. Devastated, he turned to the crowd and began to convey the full extent of the hat's complete and utter emptiness, and that's when the four Mels popped out.

You almost had the watch but didn't grab it
(DID-n't GRAB it)

And now it has been stolen by a rabbit
(BIG white RAB-bit)
He's fluffy and long eared
And now he's disappeared
So you can stand here moping in despair
(DEEP despair)
Or get in the hat and find that HARE!

POOF!

A billowy puff of smoke burst from the hat, and when it vanished, the Mels were gone.

"I don't know why, but bad ideas just sound better in song form," Cuphead said.

And without another word, he, Mugman, and Ms. Chalice dived into the hat.

17

A MIRROR-ACULOUS DISCOVERY

Now, had this been a regular hat, there wouldn't have been nearly enough room for the three of them. But magical hats tend to be as roomy as you need them to be, so the minute they jumped inside, it became as wide as a tunnel. It even felt like a tunnel, all cold and black and empty. They plunged and plunged and plunged through the darkness until, eventually, they saw a round circle that looked exactly like the opening of Hopus's hat. Cuphead was the first to fall through it, and when he arrived, he noticed two things: They were not inside the tent anymore, and there was a banana peel on top of his head.

If these seem like curious discoveries, it's because the round hole he'd seen coming at him wasn't the opening to the hat at all—it was the opening to a garbage can in the alley behind the midway.

Cuphead thought a garbage can was a strange place

to put an exit from a magical realm. Then again, magical realms were pretty strange places to begin with. He was just glad to be back on solid ground, and he intended to stay there.

And so he did—for about two seconds.

Suddenly, Mugman emerged from the exit, lifting his brother on his shoulders.

"Cuphead, *CUUUUP*-head, where are you?"

"Up here, goofball," Cuphead said.

"What are you doing up there?" asked Mugman.

And that's when Ms. Chalice popped up. The three stood there, stacked on top of one another like wobbly building blocks sticking out of a garbage can. Ms. Chalice sniffed the air.

"I don't want to be rude, but I think it's time to clean that hat."

Then, in one great heap, the three-headed tower tumbled out of the can. They had no idea how they were going to find Hopus. Fortunately, Mugman spotted a clue.

"There's Hopus," he said, pointing to Hopus. (Some clues are easier to spot than others.)

"Well, look what the hat dragged in!" the rabbit

shouted, and let out a weird, demented laugh. "Don't worry, I'm not angry—just hoppin' mad!"

And with another, even more disturbing laugh, he hopped and bounced and bounded down the alley and through the backdoor of a creepy, old building. The friends went in after him—and gasped.

It was a natural reaction, since the first thing they saw was the last thing they expected—themselves.

Wherever they looked, in every direction, there was an endless maze of Cupheads and Mugmen and Ms. Chalices.

"I think we're in the house of mirrors," Ms. Chalice said. "Let's spread out and look for Hopus."

"Good idea," said Cuphead. "Ms. Chalices, you go that way. Mugmen, you go that way. All you Cupheads, come with me."

"Right!" the reflections answered, and they all headed off in their various directions.

Though Mugman would never admit it, he was uneasy about leaving Cuphead and Ms. Chalice. After all, he wouldn't be facing just one magical rabbit; he'd be facing dozens of them. Fortunately, he had help—he was surrounded by himself, which for some reason, made him feel better. He was working his way through the maze when he heard a noise and saw a blurry figure shoot across the mirrors. He told himself it was nothing to worry about; it could have been anything... anything with a blue tuxedo and long white ears.

"He can't get all of us, boys," he told the Mugmen. "All we have to do is stick together."

When he looked in the mirrors, the Mugmen were gone.

"Cowards!" he yelled.

Of course, the worst part wasn't that he had been deserted by his own gutless reflections. The worst part was that he couldn't go with them.

Mugman continued the search, but he'd never felt more alone.

• • • • •

Meanwhile, in another part of the maze, Cuphead was inspecting the troops.

"All right, men. We've got a big job ahead of us, so we've got to be at our best. Atten-*shun*!"

All the reflections stood at attention.

"You there," he said, "suck in that gut."

The reflection took a deep breath and held it. Cuphead began to pace.

"Now, remember, you're all Cupheads, so I expect you to act like Cupheads."

Instantly, the reflections put their thumbs in their ears like moose antlers, stuck out their tongues, and made annoying raspberry noises.

"That's more like it," Cuphead said.

Just then, there was a clatter from another part of the maze. All the Cupheads turned and looked.

"Let's go," said the real Cuphead, and they all ran toward it.

● ● ● ● ●

As it happened, the commotion came from the part of the maze where Ms. Chalice was searching. When Cuphead and Mugman arrived, they found her standing with her back pressed tightly against the glass.

"He's in there," she whispered.

The brothers peeked down the line of mirrors. Sure enough, there was Hopus. In fact, there was a room full of Hopuses. This was a problem since it was impossible to tell which one the real magician was. Or was it?

Suddenly, Ms. Chalice got an idea. She reached into her pocket and pulled out the red crayon she'd been holding when Cuphead yanked her over to the window during their escape from school.

"Good thing I didn't drop this!" she said cheerfully.

And she was right. Armed with the crayon, Ms. Chalice dashed through the maze, scribbling as she went. Whenever she found a rabbit reflection, she wrote the word *Mirror* on the glass so that they'd know it wasn't real. In no time at all, there were *Mirror* markings as far as the eye could see. Still, there was something strange about one of the reflections—it was furrier and more three-dimensional than the others.

"Uh-oh," said Ms. Chalice. And in the middle of the rabbit's forehead, she wrote the word *Hare*.

Hopus rolled his eyes upward, peering up at the bright-red letters. He frowned. Quickly, he snatched the crayon from Ms. Chalice's hand and changed the word from *Hare* to *Harebrained*.

He seemed pleased.

And with a laugh that sounded a lot like a hyena with a bad case of the hiccups, he hopped swiftly through the maze and ran out of the building.

"After him!" Cuphead said.

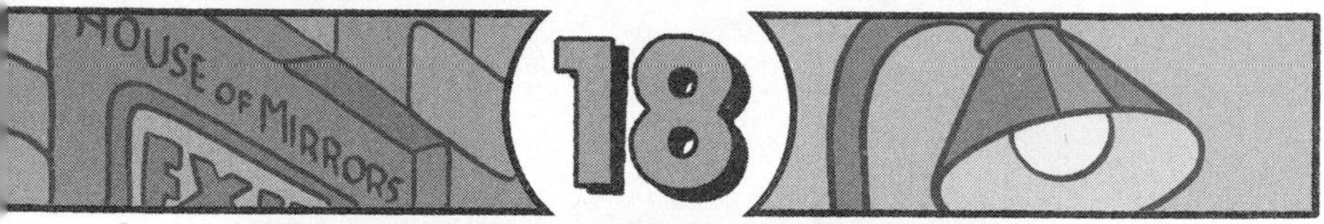
HOUSE OF MIRRORS

18

THE TORTOISES AND THE HARE

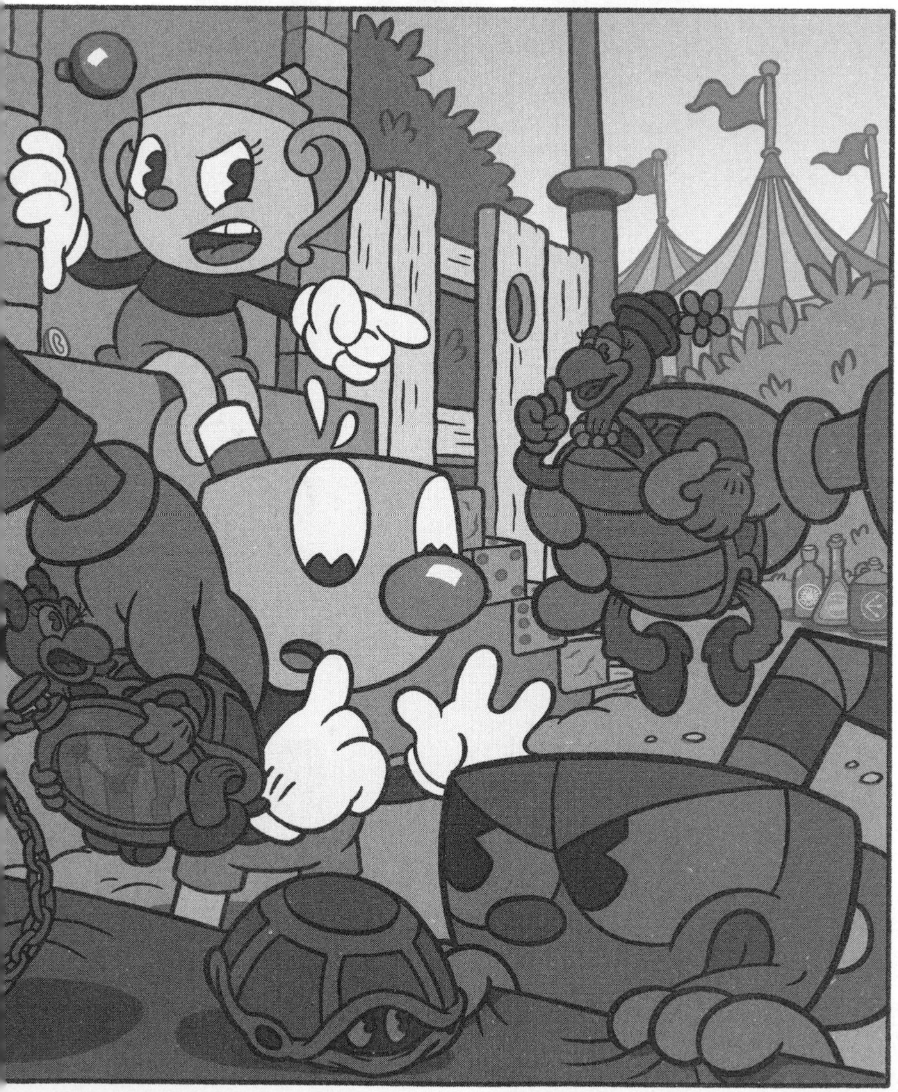

M ore determined than ever, Cuphead, Mugman, and Ms. Chalice burst out the back door. At the end of the alley was a small, handwritten sign hung between two posts. It said TRY YOUR LUCK.

"This can't be good," said Ms. Chalice.

The three of them walked up to a small table covered by a white cloth directly beneath the sign.

"Ah, customers!" Hopus exclaimed.

"Just give us the watch, Hopus," Cuphead said.

The magician smiled.

"Oh, I'll be glad to," he told them in the most sincere-sounding lie they'd heard all day. "Only I can't seem to remember which shell I put it under."

"Shell?" Mugman asked.

In a flash, Hopus produced three green shells and laid them out on the tablecloth. He then shuffled them back and forth at blinding speed so that no shell ever stayed in one place long enough for the shell watchers to get used to it.

"My friends, you see before you three shells," Hopus spieled. "Under one of them is the watch. All you have to do is pick the right one and that terrific timepiece is yours to take home. What could be easier? Go ahead, pal, give it a try."

Cuphead scratched his chin.

"You mean all I've gotta do is pick a shell?"

"That's it," said the rabbit. "Easy peasy with extra cheesy!"

Again, his hands moved swiftly around the table, clanking the shells down with a series of noisy clunks.

"Now then, which shell has the watch?"

Cuphead, Mugman, and Ms. Chalice huddled for a moment. Cuphead turned and stared at the table.

"The one in the middle," he said.

"This one?" the rabbit asked, pointing to the middle shell. Cuphead nodded.

"You're sure you wouldn't rather choose this one?" he asked, pointing to one on the end.

"Well..."

"Or this one?" he asked, pointing to the other end.

"No, no, you're not going to trick me. It's the middle one...isn't it?" Cuphead said.

Hopus grinned.

"Well, let's find out."

At that moment, all three shells sprouted arms and legs and heads and tails, which is what happens when you play with turtle shells.

"All right, gals," Hopus said. "Which one of you has the watch?"

Sure enough, the middle turtle reached into her shell and pulled out the watch.

"We win!" Mugman cheered, and it looked like they had every reason to celebrate.

But the magician still had one card up his sleeve.

On Hopus's signal, the turtles began switching shells. They were pulling them off like undershirts and replacing them with the one that belonged to the turtle next door. They switched again and again and again until Cuphead had no idea which shell was hiding the watch.

"Every player makes the same mistake," Hopus howled. "They're watching the hare when they ought to be watching the tortoise! Ha-ha-ha-ha-ha!"

While the rabbit stood there cackling like some long-eared chuckle machine, Cuphead decided he'd had enough of this game. He looked at the turtles.

"Grab 'em," he said.

Mugman and Ms. Chalice lunged at the table, but the little green watch thieves scattered.

"They're getting away!" Ms. Chalice yelled, which is something you don't hear very often about turtles, but maybe you should.

You see, turtles are much faster than given credit for, and that's especially true of the ones on the Inkwell Isles. (The locals called them "green lightning.") These three ran like world-class sprinters, leaving little streaks of smoke behind as they disappeared up the alley, down the path, and over the fence.

"You go that way, you go that way, and I'll go this way," Cuphead said. "Follow those turtles!"

And that's how the trio of them ended up heading out in three different directions on the trail of the tortoises. If only they'd known where it would lead them.

19

A DANCE WITH DANGER

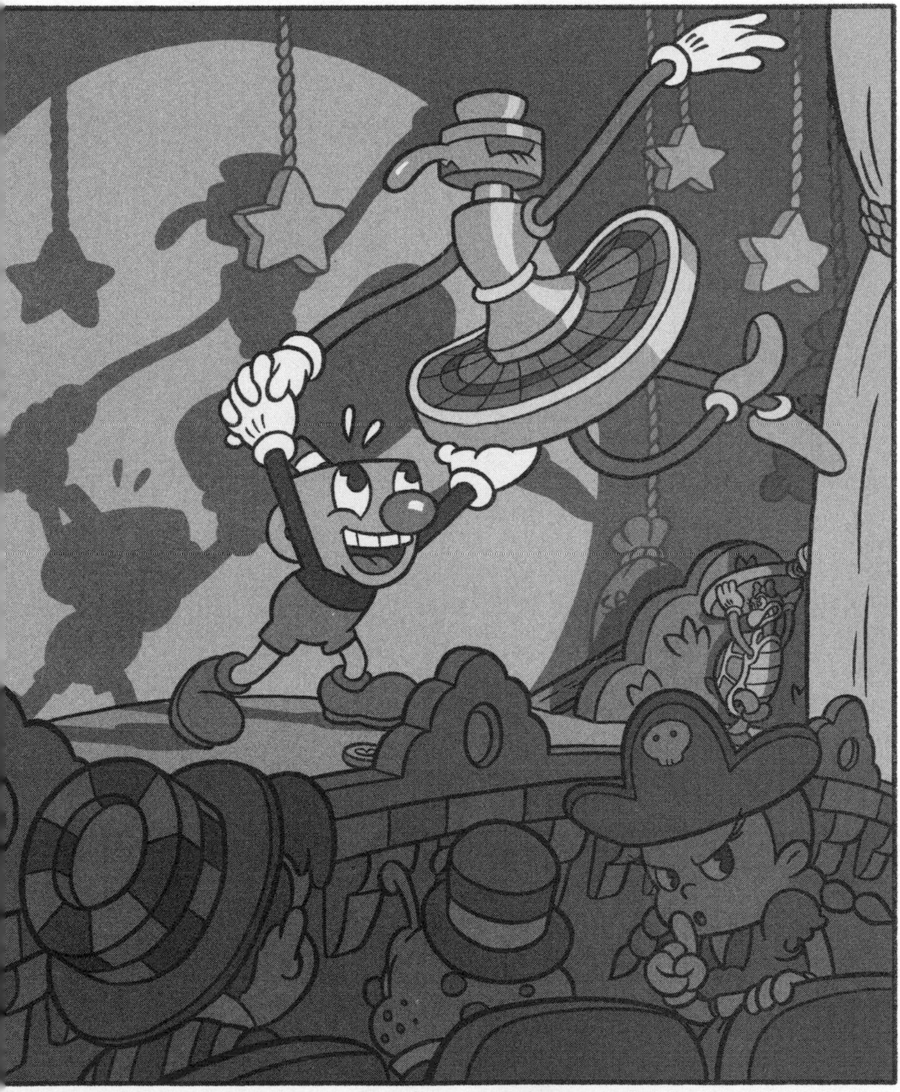

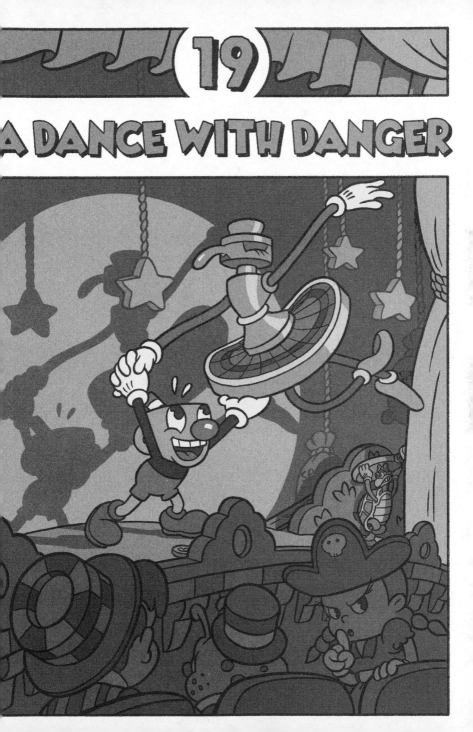

Mugman chased one of the turtles down an aisle that led back to the midway. The rowdy reptile (who was as tricky as she was fast) crawled under the side of a large, colorful tent. Mugman crawled in right behind her. When he emerged, he found himself at a performance unlike anything he could imagine.

It was a ballet. He'd heard of ballets, of course, but never expected to see one (at least not at a carnival in a tent he'd secretly sneaked into while chasing a watch-stealing turtle—that seemed like the kind of thing that happened to other people). Still, here he was, and now that he'd seen it with his own eyes, he understood the appeal. The music was enchanting—like something you'd hear in only the fanciest elevators—but the most wonderful part was what was happening up on the stage.

Pirouletta was dancing. Actually, she wasn't just dancing—she was pirouetting.

Pirouletta was a good ballerina, but a great pirouetter. The greatest pirouetter in the whole world, according to signs posted all over the tent, and Mugman believed it. As a wheel, she was perfectly balanced, and could whirl and twirl like a shiny gold tornado. He was mesmerized.

Watching the performance, it occurred to him that ballet was a little bit like flying. It was smooth and graceful, and there were moments when Pirouletta seemed to defy gravity. The fact that she could hover that way without a propeller was nothing short of amazing, and he was green with envy. Well, not actually green, like a tree or an avocado or that little lady in the audience, but more like—

Little lady in the audience? The turtle!

What was he thinking? Mugman had completely forgotten about the turtle. The hard-shelled hoodlum was standing near the front of the crowd, and when she saw Mugman, she climbed onto the stage and made a break for it. Mugman went after her.

But there was a problem—he was on the opposite

side of the stage. Crossing it in the middle of a ballet wouldn't be easy. Still, he had to try.

Very quietly, while Pirouletta danced and leaped and twirled, Mugman tiptoed across the back of the stage. Well, halfway across.

The audience howled.

Of course, the right thing to do would've been to just keep moving. But Mugman couldn't move. He was experiencing a sensation he'd never felt before—stage fright. And the minute he looked out into the crowd and saw all those faces staring back at him, he froze.

As he stood there, staring and sweating, the laughter got louder and louder. But not everyone thought it was funny.

"No one interrupts my performance!" Pirouletta huffed.

She glared at him with eyes as hard as her metal tutu. He tried to explain, but before he could get a word out, Pirouletta had pulled him into one of her spectacular spins. Mugman twirled round and round like a top until he was flung—with the grace of a nauseous swan—back to the wrong side of the stage.

When he was able, he stood up again. He felt dizzy,

humiliated, and strangely enough, a little bit brave. Not a lot, mind you, but enough to try again. After all, it was almost time for Elder Kettle's party, and the turtle was getting away.

So he dusted himself off, took a deep breath, and stepped back out onto the stage. This time, he deliberately didn't look at the audience to avoid getting stage fright. Unfortunately, he did look at Pirouletta and got regular fright. She was enraged. He watched as she made several long, swooping leaps in the air, getting higher and higher with each lunge, and just when she was about to put her foot where he kept his face—

Mugman caught her. He didn't know why; it was a reflex. Still, it was a good catch, beautifully executed, and the audience applauded. Well, if anything, this made Pirouletta even angrier. She spun away from him, then back again, her foot whirling toward him like the blade of a propeller. Mugman ducked and dodged, but he did it so gracefully that the crowd never even suspected he feared for his life. To them, it looked like dancing, a glorious punching, kicking, twirling, tossing ballet by two masters of the craft. Finally, an infuriated Pirouletta grabbed hold of Mugman and the pair spun in an elegant, entangled brawl to every corner of the stage.

When the twirling stopped, and you could again tell one dancer from the other, Mugman was holding Pirouletta above his head in majestic suspension. How it happened, he had no idea. But since it occurred just as the music came to a rousing conclusion, the audience exploded in wild applause. They were cheering and whistling and throwing flowers. Pirouletta, who was completely surprised by the reaction, walked to the edge of the stage and made a deep curtsy. And Mugman, not wanting to seem rude, did the same.

Considering this was his first ballet, he felt like it had gone pretty well. He thought about staying longer (the crowd was begging for an encore), but he had a turtle to catch. So he did what any artist would do in his position: He picked up a flower, put it in his teeth, and made a great, noble leap off the end of the stage.

And he kept right on leaping until he'd danced his way out the back of the tent.

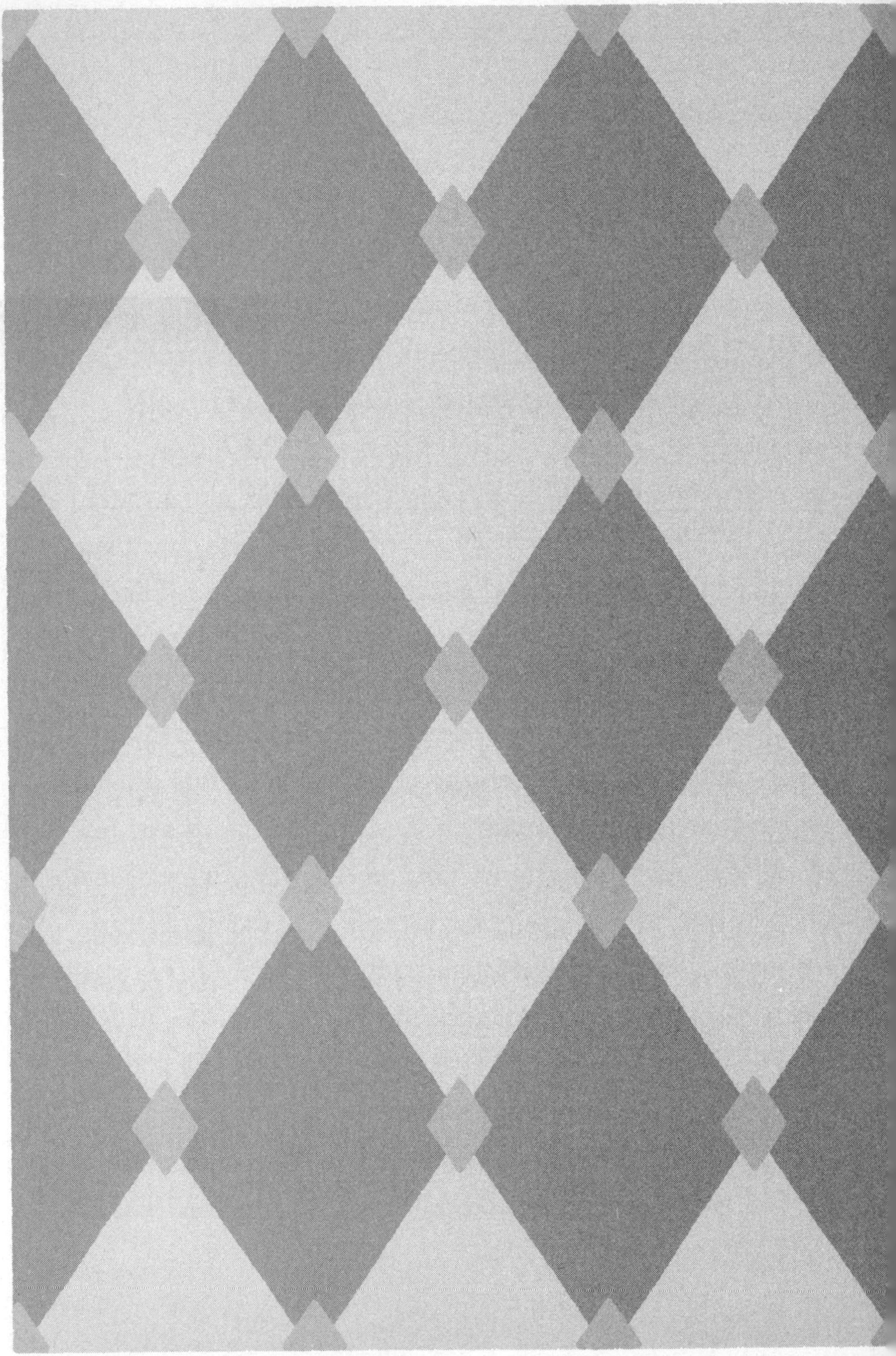

20

SIGNS AND CYMBALS

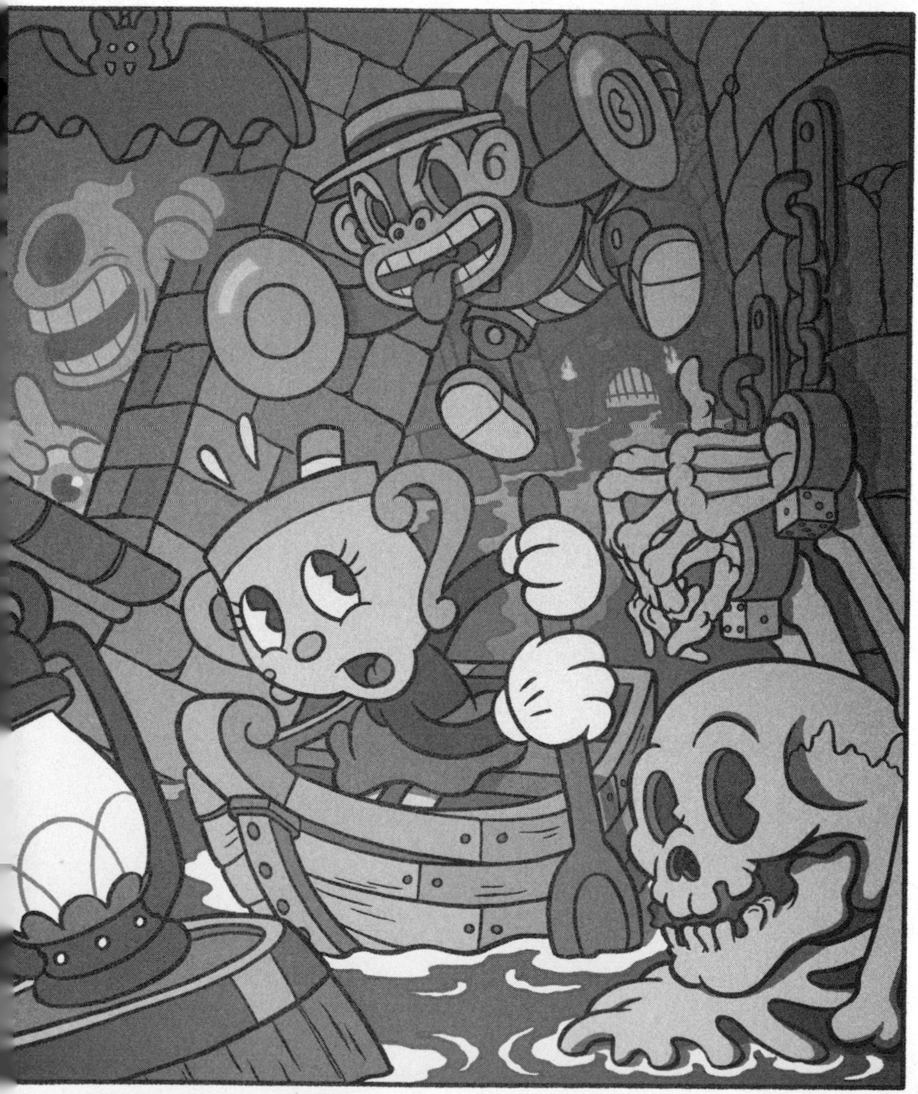

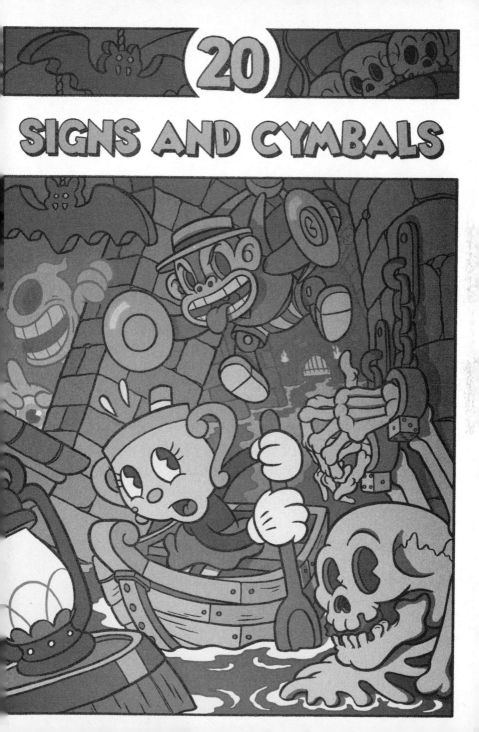

Meanwhile, Ms. Chalice (whose chase had taken her in the opposite direction from Mugman) was busy tracking turtle-size footprints that led to the dark end of the midway. This was not the nice, bright, cheery side of the carnival, where they sold cotton candy and malted milk mush. This was the creepy, crawly side where they sold critter candy and un-malted milk mush. She got chills just being here.

Still, she was determined to find the fugitive turtle and, with a little luck, get Elder Kettle's watch back in time for the surprise party. To do that, she'd go almost anywhere.

The tracks took her down a twisted, winding pathway—and that's where they stopped. Which, by the process of deduction (Ms. Chalice had read many detective stories, and knew all about deduction), meant the turtle must be right here. There were only two problems with that theory: The turtle was not here, and what was here was nothing Ms. Chalice wanted to find.

It was a gigantic clown's mouth. Whether it was attached to some gigantic clown, she had no idea, but it wouldn't have surprised her (this was, after all, the dark side). All she really knew was that she was standing beside a row of tiny, boats that took you into the big, gruesome mouth, and from there—well, the possibilities were really too disturbing to think about.

She looked around. Up above the painted clown face was a crooked, decrepit-looking sign that said FUNHOUSE. This puzzled Ms. Chalice. It certainly didn't look fun. And from the screams coming from inside, it didn't sound fun. She thought perhaps the sign used to say NOT FUNHOUSE and some of the letters had fallen off, which would have made a lot more sense. But to be honest, the funhouse sign wasn't really the thing that bothered her. What bothered her were all the other signs, the ones that said DANGER and WARNING and BEWARE and ENTER AT YOUR OWN RISK and THIS MEANS YOU, MS. CHALICE and VISIT OUR GIFT SHOP (their prices were frighteningly high). She was about to give up the search altogether when something entering the tunnel caught her eye. It was one of the tiny boats—and sticking out of it like a periscope was a skinny green turtle head.

And even though it seemed like the worst idea she'd had in a very long time, Ms. Chalice caught the next boat to clown town.

As she floated through the enormous mouth, a spine-tingling laugh echoed off the walls. The next thing she knew, she was headed into a pit of total darkness.

"This place gives me the heebie-jeebies," she said. "And not in a good way."

She moved slowly down the narrow river, listening to the horrible eeks and shrieks roaring through the tunnel. In the shadows, she could see spiderwebs, ghostly figures, and ghouls carefully placed to give the ride a haunted feel. But mostly, she kept her eye on the boat ahead of her—the one she desperately needed to catch.

Just then, she saw a display that looked like a mechanical witch stirring a cauldron with a big wooden spoon.

"Mind if I borrow this?" she said, plucking the giant stirrer from the witch's hands. "Thanks!"

And sure enough, by using the spoon as a paddle, she was able to close the gap between her boat and the turtle's. Well, she must've made the turtle pretty nervous, because the instant they reached the next scary scene, the turtle jumped out of her boat and hid herself among the gravestone markers and devilish scarecrows.

Ms. Chalice sighed and followed her.

"Little turtle!" she yelled into the darkness. "Come out, come out, wherever you are!"

A few feet away, she saw something move. It could've been the turtle, but since it was in the shadows, it was impossible to tell. She took a step forward, then another, then another and—

CLA-AAA-ANG!

A pair of big, shiny cymbals crashed together just inches from her head.

It was Mr. Chimes!

Of course, Ms. Chalice had already met Mr. Chimes once that day. He was the hollow-eyed windup monkey playing a street organ in front of the carnival gate. She hadn't liked the looks of him then, and she liked them even less now.

"Eek! Eek! Eek!" Mr. Chimes screeched, then disappeared back into the darkness.

Ms. Chalice's ears were ringing. In fact, it felt like someone was banging a gong inside her head.

"You better not do that again," she called out. "I mean it. You don't want to monkey around with me."

Wherever Mr. Chimes was, Ms. Chalice hoped he was listening. The last thing she needed today was to have her head squashed by a band instrument.

Just then, the turtle leaped out from behind a gravestone marked B. WARE and ran into a spooky grove of cardboard trees. Ms. Chalice went in after her. Carefully, she checked behind each trunk hoping to find the turtle, and hoping not to find—

CLA-AAAAANG!

Out of the branches came Mr. Chimes! The terrible brass cymbals chomped at her like crocodile jaws.

CLA-AAAAANG! CLA-AAAAANG! CLA-AAAAANG!

Ms. Chalice moved out of the way just in time, narrowly escaping a head squashing.

"I'm warning you!" she said again. "I don't want to play right now!"

But Mr. Chimes was gone.

Suddenly, the turtle made a break for it. Ms. Chalice raced down the tunnel after the turtle until she came to a haunted holiday scene. It was filled with eerie, terrible-looking toys. There were toy soldiers with twisted faces and creepy, grinning dolls. And in the very center was a gigantic jack-in-the-box playing a mournful tune.

Doo-DO-doo-DO-dum-dum-dum-dum-DOO.

Ms. Chalice moved as quietly as a mouse on a stack of pillows. Carefully, she approached the giant box. Without warning, Mr. Chimes burst out from behind it!

"Eek! Eek! Eek!"

But when he looked for Ms. Chalice, she was gone. The music slowed to a crawl—

DOO...dum...doo...doo....SPROINNNNNNNG!

The door on the jack-in-the-box burst open. But instead of a terrifying clown, out popped...Ms. Chalice.

CLA-AAAANG!

She brought two trash can lids together on each side of Mr. Chimes's head. He wobbled and bobbled like a top looking for a place to fall, then toppled headfirst into one of the passing boats. It carried him down the tunnel.

"I told you I didn't want to play right now," Ms. Chalice called after him. "But ask me again later. This was fun!"

Out of the corner of her eye, she saw a little green streak dashing out the end of the tunnel.

She sighed.

A turtle chaser's work is never done.

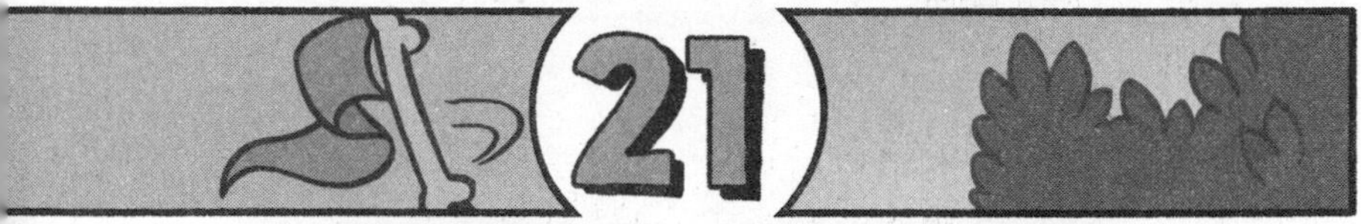

21

HORSIN' AROUND AND AROUND

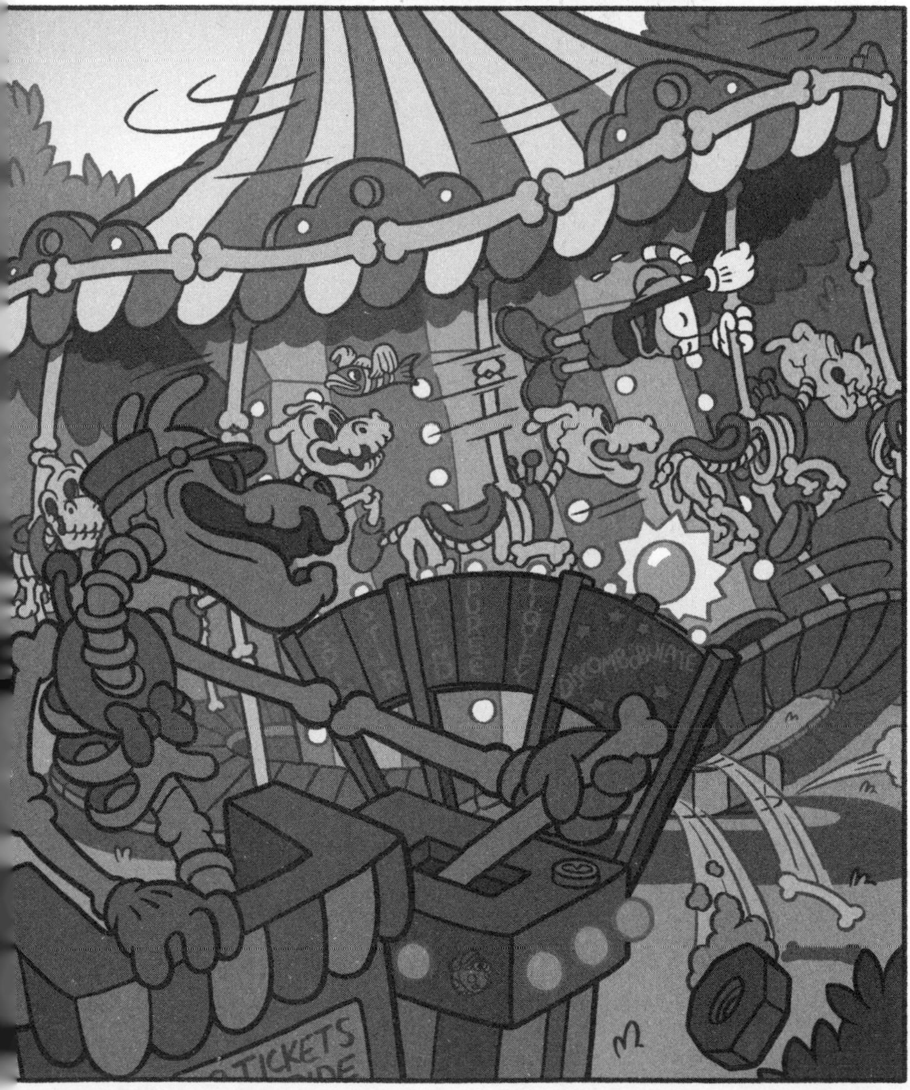
TICKETS

Now, while Mugman and Ms. Chalice were off having their adventures, Cuphead had been busy chasing down the third turtle from Hopus's game—and not very successfully. It was like pursuing a green, leathery cheetah in a rocket-powered shell. Not only was the turtle fast; she was crafty. Whenever Cuphead would manage to gain on her, she'd weave through the crowd—bounding over handbags, swinging on neckties, racing through a maze of legs—and give him the slip. Finally, they came to an open space and Cuphead saw the turtle running toward a curious-looking contraption. He ran after her.

The contraption turned out to be, well . . . Cuphead wasn't really sure what it was. In some ways, it looked like a carousel, which is to say it did the things that carousels do. But if you came to it hoping to find painted ponies and bouncy, cheerful music, you would be deeply disappointed.

It wasn't that kind of carnival, and this was not that kind of ride.

"Jeepers," Cuphead said to himself.

He stared at the mysterious attraction. The decorative outer rim was made of bones. The poles were made of bones. Every single horse was made of bones.

"Climb aboard," a terrible voice said. "You're just in time."

Cuphead turned and looked at the ride operator, a skeleton horse wearing a green visor and red bow tie. (He was also made of bones.)

"The name's Phear Lap," the operator said. "Welcome to the Scary-Go-Round."

Cuphead gulped.

"Um . . . I was just looking for someone. But I think he went somewhere else."

Phear Lap pulled a handle, and an eerie tune oozed from a speaker. A moment later, the repulsive ride crept slowly around—and there was the turtle, gently bobbing up and down on the back of one of the bony ponies. Both horse and rider turned and gave Cuphead an evil grin.

"Enjoy the ride," Phear Lap said.

Cuphead took a nervous step forward. He didn't feel good about this. For one thing, the ride didn't look healthy—in fact, it looked downright malnourished. What if it collapsed? What if it was haunted? What if a giant dog came along and buried the whole thing in the backyard? There was a lot to think about, but unfortunately, he didn't have the time. Elder Kettle's party was in less than an hour, and he'd been through too much today to turn back now.

"Are these good horses?" he asked.

"Real thorough-deads," Phear Lap said.

Surprisingly, that didn't help.

Cuphead steadied himself, picked out the least nightmarish mare he could find, and jumped. Luckily, the horse he landed on was not far from the turtle. He reached out for her, but the bone-riding buckaroo quickly moved to another mount. The chase was on. Cuphead stood up on the back of his horse (he'd seen this done in cowboy pictures a hundred times) and made a magnificent leap onto another saddle. The turtle moved again. Cuphead followed. And so it went, with the two of them jumping around the ride like two kings on an undead checkerboard. Finally, the turtle had had enough. She ducked her head inside her shell and plunged off the ride onto the pavement. The shell bounced, skidded, rolled, and eventually stopped. The turtle immediately popped back out and began running away. Which meant it was time for Cuphead to make his own leap from the Scary-Go-Round, and just when he was about to—

VRRRRROOOOOMMMMM!

Everything got faster.

"Hold on tight," Phear Lap wheezed. "It's going to be a bumpy ride."

The whole contraption spun like a record player set to high speed. Even the music was faster. The horse Cuphead was riding bucked and writhed, twisting in all directions. Cuphead hugged the pole as tightly as he could as the world outside the ride became nothing but a blur.

"Stop!" he yelled.

"What's that? You say you want to go faster?" Phear Lap wheezed. "Well, anything you say."

He reached down and grabbed the lever in front of

him. On it were marked the words *SPIN*, *STIR*, *BLEND*, *PUREE*, *LIQUEFY*, and *DISCOMBOBULATE*. He pushed the lever to the very end.

Suddenly, the killer carousel turned round and round so fast it looked like the inside of a washing machine. It was impossible to tell where one horse started and the other ended. And if that weren't bad enough (and it almost certainly was), a band of skeleton outlaws fell from the roof and landed on the bone horses. They surrounded Cuphead, and one of them threw a rope around him, and just when it looked like this would be the end—

Cuphead escaped. How, you ask? Well, it wasn't easy. But as luck would have it, Cuphead was a regular listener and big-time fan of the *Wyatt Burp: Rootin' Tootin' Root Beer Mug* radio program. As you know, Wyatt was constantly getting into jams involving outlaws, and he always managed to get the best of them. Fortunately, Cuphead had heard all 527 episodes, including the 43 that dealt specifically with skeleton outlaws, and the 11 involving creepy carousels. Anyway, it goes without saying that, with that kind of background, it was a simple matter of using what he'd learned to turn the tables on the bad guys. Explaining it would be much too complicated; you'd be far better off listening to the Wyatt Burp broadcasts yourself, and then it will all make perfect sense.

But for now, the important thing to know is that Cuphead burst out of the spinning Scary-Go-Round still riding his skeleton horse, and it was a very impressive sight. The two of them knocked over Phear Lap as they galloped past him in pursuit of the turtle, and they never looked back.

Now, as it happened, this particular skeleton horse was every bit as fast as he was disgusting, so they were able to gain a lot of ground in practically no time at all. They weaved through the crowd with Cuphead gripping the reins and guiding the horse this way and that way. Then, when Cuphead looked to his right, he saw a turtle running down a side path. And when he looked to his left, he saw another turtle running down another side path. It was all very confusing until he noticed that Ms. Chalice and Mugman were trailing along behind them.

"Whoa!" Cuphead yelled, pulling back on the reins. The horse locked down his hooves and they slid to a stop.

"Look over there!" Ms. Chalice said. They all did.

It was the third turtle, the one Cuphead had been chasing. She was standing in the center of the midway holding out Elder Kettle's watch. (Cuphead made a mental note never to trust a turtle—they were nothing but shells and sticky fingers.) But the worst part was, she wasn't alone.

22

CUPHEAD'S CURSE

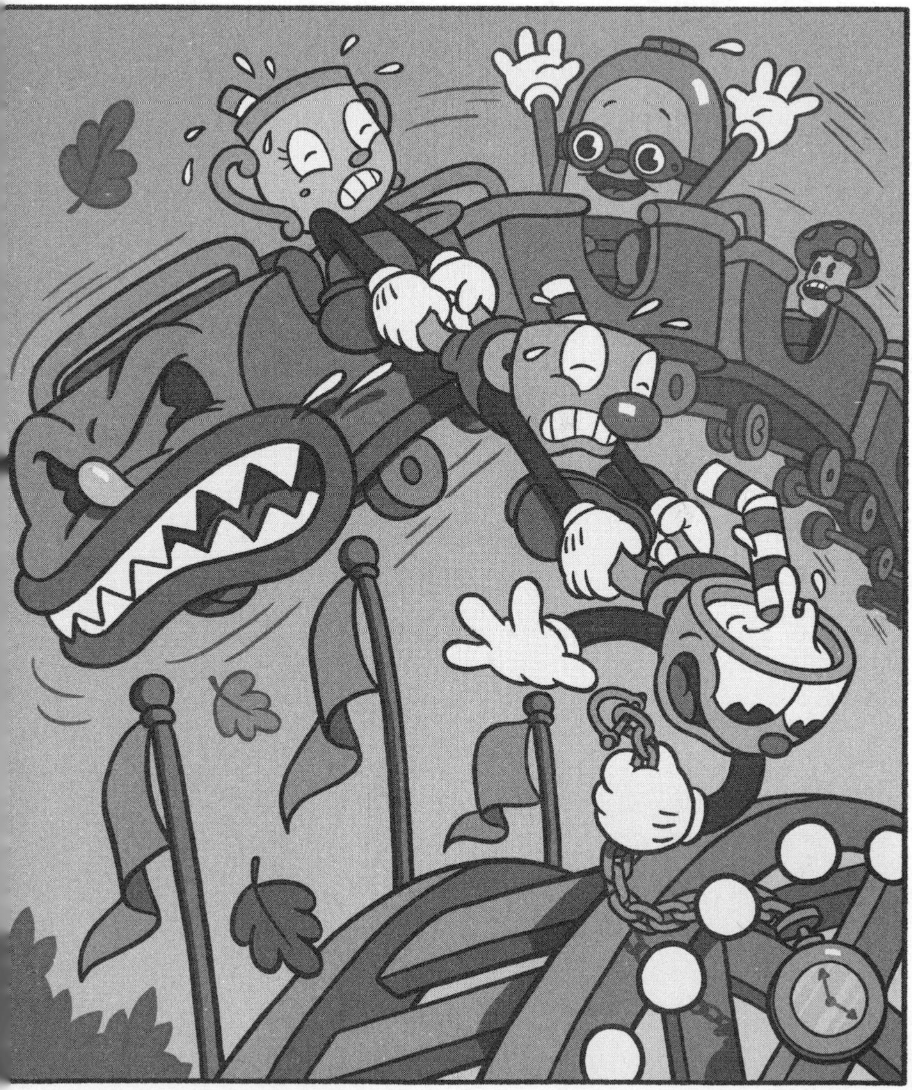

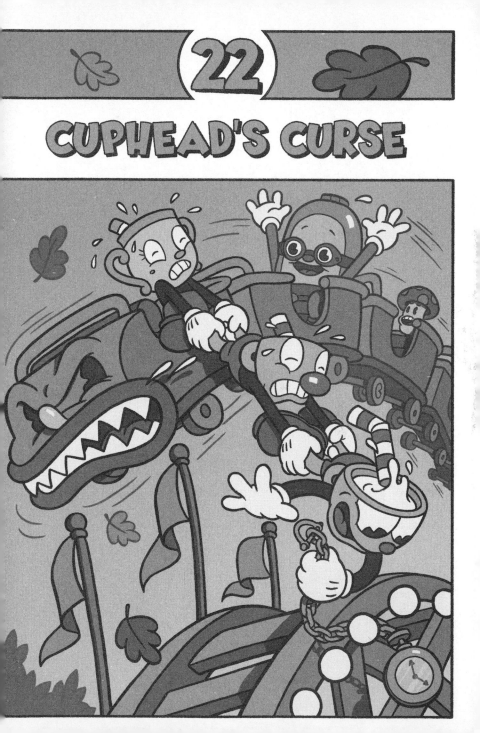

Standing alongside the turtle was a regular who's who of hoodlumism. Everyone was there: Beppi the Clown, Brineybeard, Hopus Pocus, Djimmi the Great, Sally Stageplay, Cala Maria, Mr. Chimes, and the cigar-chomping, derby-wearing duck who had stolen the watch in the first place. Beppi reached down and took the precious treasure from the turtle.

"So, we meet again," Beppi said to the trio. He handed the watch to the duck. "Take this. You know what to do."

The duck nodded. Then he looked at Cuphead.

"Don't feel bad, kid. It's only a year until your friend's *next* birthday," he said. "And you know what they say—time flies!"

It was an excruciating pun (the Odd Ducks would've loved it), but it was also true. Time really did fly, and the blabbering bird intended to prove it.

He tucked the magnificent timepiece under his derby and carried it high into the air. Then, in the ultimate insult, he left it in the one place where Cuphead could never, ever get to it.

He hung it from the very highest point on the Dizzy Borden!

Cuphead gasped.

"Well, what are you waiting for?" said Beppi. "Go get it—unless you're scared!"

Scared? Cuphead didn't know the meaning of the word. Then he took a long look at the Dizzy Borden and realized he was willing to learn.

The Dizzy Borden was a sleek, sinister roller coaster that zoomed around a looping, twisting, stomach-turning track. It reached heights that would give a mountain goat a nosebleed. It was dangerous. It was evil. It was rage on a rail.

And speaking of rage...

"Who you callin' scared?" Ms. Chalice seethed. "We ain't scared of nothin'!"

The nerve of some people. Ms. Chalice wasn't about to let some smart-alecky clown tell her what she could or couldn't do. So without so much as a by-your-leave, she grabbed Cuphead and Mugman by their collars and pulled them toward the roller coaster.

Cuphead couldn't believe this was happening. His master plan was falling apart. From the very beginning, Elder Kettle's birthday had been his excuse for *not* going on the roller coaster. And now his birthday present was the thing forcing him *onto* the beast? It couldn't be! Fate would not be that cruel.

"We'll show them who's scared," Ms. Chalice muttered. "And that know-it-all frog better stay out of our way, too."

Frog? Of course, the frog! Cuphead's eyes lit up. In order to ride the roller coaster, they'd have to get past R. U. Bigenuf, the measuring frog. There was still a chance!

R. U. Bigenuf was a large sign that looked like a frog wearing a polka-dot vest and a blue tailcoat. There was one posted outside every ride at the carnival. If you were taller than R. U.'s outstretched hand, that meant you could go on the ride. But if you were shorter, you'd have to wait until you were "Bigenuf."

Cuphead thought the shortest, squatiest thoughts he could think.

"Holy mackerel!" Mugman said, and he gave a long whistle.

They had arrived at the Dizzy Borden. The massive track towered above them, blocking out the sun and significantly dimming their hopes of a pain-free future.

Cuphead pulled away from Ms. Chalice and waltzed right up to R. U. Bigenuf, glorious protector of the short and stumpy. He held his breath and moved in close to the sign, and though it was by only the smallest part of an inch, he just fit underneath R. U.'s hand.

"You are *NOT* Bigenuf," the sign said.

Cuphead couldn't contain himself.

"Yay!" he said, leaping into the air.

Unfortunately, he made his leap while he was still standing under the sign. His head bonked against R. U.'s hand, causing a tiny little lump to sprout. And while it wasn't a very big lump—

"You *ARE* Bigenuf. Congratulations!"

—it added just enough height to put him on the ride. Defeat had been snatched from the jaws of victory, and there was absolutely nothing he could do about it.

"Come on, boys," Ms. Chalice said. "We've got to go pick up our watch."

Pick up their watch? Had she just said, *pick up their watch*? Like it was something in Porkrind's store instead of the most terrible, treacherous place in the world? Because if that's what she said, then Cuphead had news for her—she was right.

They did have to go pick up their watch.

He didn't know if it was Ms. Chalice's words or the fact that he'd recently received a blow to the head from the wise and helpful R. U. Bigenuf (who was about so much more than measuring), but he suddenly realized that he'd been looking at this all wrong. It wasn't about the roller coaster; it was about the watch. It had *always* been about the watch. Because as bad as this ride might be (and he was expecting something between a disaster and a tragedy), showing up at Elder Kettle's party without a birthday gift would be even worse.

Besides, he couldn't let his friends go up there alone. They needed him. (And they'd never let him live it down.) So with their mission settled and their fate sealed, the three of them locked arms and marched out to meet the infamous Dizzy Borden.

It would be a meeting none of them would ever forget.

When they reached the loading platform, Dizzy was there waiting for them.

"Oh good. Three new victims...I mean, er, riders," the train said. "Now watch your step. I wouldn't want anything *BAD* to happen to you."

Then it let out a laugh so chilling Cuphead thought they might have to wait for the spring thaw. Of all the villains they'd met in this place, nothing compared to the Dizzy Borden.

They climbed into their seats.

As soon as he sat down, Cuphead saw a seat belt with a silver buckle. He reached for it. It moved. He reached again, it moved again, and this time it retreated inside the seat and refused to come back out.

The Dizzy Borden gave a low, guttural growl.

"Everyone comfy?" it asked.

"My safety belt just ran away from me," said Cuphead.

"Yes, it's shy around new people," said the train. "Ready?"

"No!" Cuphead insisted.

"Good!" yelled the train, and it took off with a burst of speed that nearly threw Cuphead out of the cart.

He held on for dear life as they roared around

the track. The train leaped through a fire ring, and spiraled through a corkscrew, and flipped upside down as they crossed a pit of hungry-looking alligators.

"Woo-hoo! Wheee!" Ms. Chalice screamed. "Isn't this fun, Cuphead?"

Cuphead screamed as well, but in a slightly different tone. You see, he was dangling from the cart like a worm on a hook as the alligators snapped at him from below.

"Help!" he yelled, and Mugman pulled him back inside.

Just in time, too. Because up ahead was the part of the ride they'd been waiting for, a skyscraping loop de loop that would take them so close to the stars they'd be able to ask for autographs. That's where they'd find Elder Kettle's watch.

The loop was a fiendishly impressive feat of irresponsible engineering, the kind of thing you'd build only if your goal were to make sure hospitals did a brisk business. As Cuphead understood it, the train would rocket around the loop three times in a row, meaning they'd have three chances to grab the watch. If they failed to reach it by the third try—well, then they would've gone through all this for nothing.

The Dizzy Borden picked up speed. First, it made a terrifying plunge, then shot up one side of the loop. Cuphead felt his eyes being pushed to the back of his head, but before that happened, he spotted the watch. It was hanging there, all gold and shimmering, just where the duck had left it. He grabbed for it as they barreled past but was a fraction of a second too late. Ms. Chalice and Mugman missed as well, and they braced themselves for the second pass.

This time, Cuphead was sure they'd get it. He got into position and leaned out at exactly the right angle. But just as he made his reach, the treacherous train whipped violently to the side, flinging him back into the cart. On the bright side, this meant Ms. Chalice could use his face as a stepping stool, a maneuver that gave her the extra length she needed to reach the chain. And she might've had it, too, if Mugman hadn't grabbed for it at precisely the same moment, and the two of them collided.

"*Ha-ha-ha-ha-ha-ha-ha-ha!*" the train laughed as the three of them lay there in a helpless, tangled heap. "Last chance. Don't blow it!"

And even though he knew the train was trying to be rude, Cuphead couldn't have agreed more.

"Last chance," he said. "Let's not blow it."

They nodded and got ready for their third go-round on the loop de loop.

This was it. The final pass. The train sneered and streaked down the track like a meteor. As they blazed toward the watch, Ms. Chalice moved to the edge of the cart—or tried to. Suddenly, her seat belt cinched up like a vise, squeezing her so tightly she could barely breathe. She tried to free herself, but it was no use. She'd been taken out of commission.

Fortunately, Cuphead and Mugman had a plan. Mugman would hold Cuphead's ankles while he leaned all the way out of the coaster and grabbed the watch. It was risky, but it had a good chance of working.

Of course, the Dizzy Borden could never allow their plan to work out so easily.

With Mugman holding and Cuphead reaching, the brothers began their acrobatic attempt. That's when the front of the train leaped into the air, causing the carts behind it to snap like a whip. Mugman lost his grip and Cuphead found himself suspended in midair. He reached out just in time to grab hold of the very last cart. The coaster whipped back and forth trying to throw him, but Cuphead held on tight. Then, when the cart jerked to the right, Cuphead swung his legs to the left and—with only the tip of his toe, mind you—snagged the chain of the watch. He quickly kicked it into his waiting hand and crawled back into the cart.

"You got it!" Ms. Chalice cheered.

"Got it?" the train said. "Well, I'll fix that!"

Furious, the Dizzy Borden headed for the most perilous part of the track—the Chopper. The Chopper was a gigantic ax that swung just over the heads of the cart riders. At least, it was *supposed* to be over their heads. This time, things would be different. As they headed toward the enormous ax, the friends felt their seats being lifted into the air. The gigantic ax was swinging toward them like a perilous pendulum!

"Everybody out!" Ms. Chalice said, and with one great lunge, they leaped out of the cart and onto the Chopper.

This was, at best, a temporary solution. When the ax swung outward, the three friends were flung into the air and out over the midway. They flew past Beppi and Brineybeard and Hopus and Sally and Djimmi and Cala Maria and Mr. Chimes and the derby-wearing duck, and kept right on going.

"After them!" Beppi said.

• • • • •

Cuphead was the first to come down. He crashed through the top of a tent, landing on a knife thrower in the middle of his act. Tragically, this caused one of his throws to go badly off course, and the knife sailed across the tent and shaved off half of Barnaby "the Human Cannonball" Muldoon's handlebar mustache. And since perfect balance is essential when you're being shot from a cannon, Barnaby's now-lopsided nose-cozy caused him to miss the net entirely and land in Ernestine Elephant's food trough.

"Oops! Sorry!" Cuphead yelled, but the Human Cannonball was not in a forgiving mood. Neither was Ernestine.

The two chased him around the tent.

• • • • •

Meanwhile, one tent over, Ms. Chalice had her own troubles. She'd come down during a performance by the Yak-robats, who were just completing their world-famous fifteen-yak pyramid (or the "Yak Stack," as they called it in the papers). Well, as you can imagine, it raised some eyebrows when a non-yak outsider landed on the very top of the pyramid. Still, it was a nice landing, and the audience cheered appreciatively, and everything might've been all right had the moment not brought out Ms. Chalice's natural showmanship.

"Ta-da!" she cried, and took a deep bow. It was the bow that did it. The tower of yaks shook, then shifted, then toppled into a pile.

"We'll get you for this!" the bottom yak groaned. And once they'd recovered, they chased her around the room.

•　•　•　•　•

As for Mugman, he didn't have the luxury of landing on a nice, soft tent. He came down on the Test-Your-Strength booth, where he landed on the lever, sent the puck shooting upward, and rung the bell.

"Congratulations, you win a tin monkey!" the booth operator said.

"This is the best day ever!" said Mugman.

And he strolled out of the booth with his prize.

•　•　•　•　•

The three of them met up again on the main aisle of the midway. Cuphead was being chased by "Half-Handlebar-Mustache" Muldoon and a hungry-looking elephant, Ms. Chalice was running from fifteen angry yaks, and Mugman was admiring his monkey. But the worst was still to come.

"There they are!" Beppi yelled, and the mob of villains rushed toward them.

"This way!" Cuphead yelled.

The three ran down the aisle until they came to a split in the path. In the confusion, Cuphead and Ms. Chalice turned left, and Mugman turned right. The villains split up and went after them.

Cuphead and Ms. Chalice looked around for a place to hide. Then Ms. Chalice spotted something even better.

"Follow me!" she said.

The two of them climbed over a railing and jumped into the seat of a bumper car.

"Do you know how to drive one of these things?" Cuphead asked.

Ms. Chalice smiled.

"Just watch me," she said.

Remember, Ms. Chalice's dream was to be a race car driver. She steered her way through the crowd of bumper cars, narrowly missing each one with her expert driving. Then—*THUD!*—something rammed them from the rear. When Cuphead turned around, he saw Djimmi the Great and Mr. Chimes in the car directly behind them. Before he could warn

Ms. Chalice—*THUD!*—a car with Brineybeard and Hopus bashed them from the side.

"Hold on," Ms. Chalice said, and turned toward the rail.

CR-RACK!

The bumper car busted through the wooden rail and went racing down the aisle.

"We've got to get Mugman," Cuphead said.

"We'll find him later," said Ms. Chalice. "Right now, we've got to get out of here."

And a few seconds later, the little bumper car headed out the front gate and onto the open road.

23

BUMPER CARNIVAL

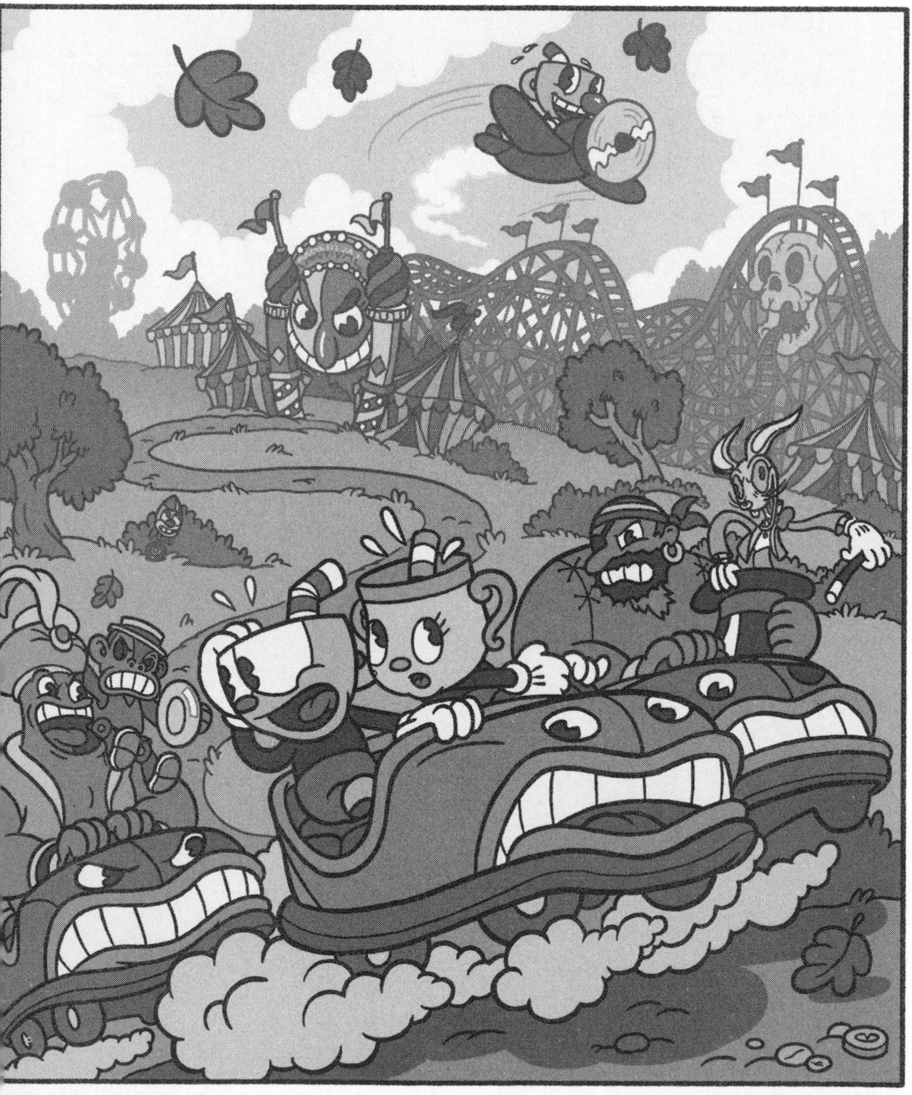

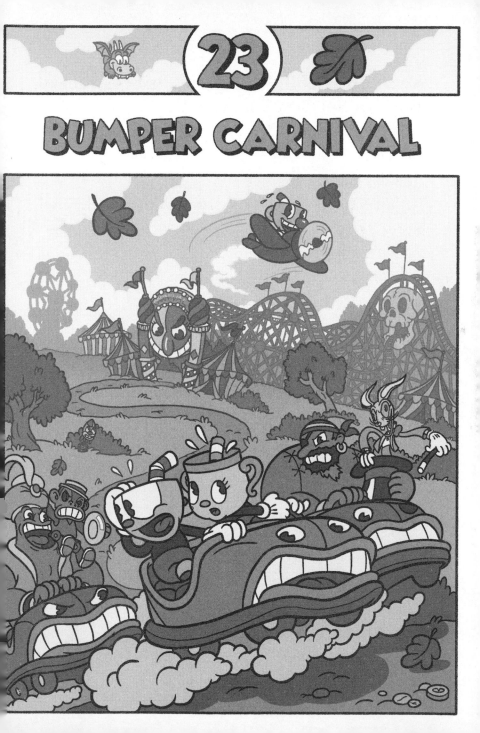

Ms. Chalice and Cuphead were driving away from the carnival in a borrowed bumper car, which was an unusual sight on the Inkwell Isles. Oh sure, maybe these things happened in the big city, but here on the isles, people were particular about the kinds of vehicles they let use their streets (those being cars, trucks, buses, wagons, bicycles, roller skates, and boats that were afraid of the water). But as embarrassed as Cuphead was by all the honking and staring, they had bigger problems.

"Holy smoke. We've got company," he said.

He didn't say it was good company, and in fact, it was the other kind. Brineybeard and Hopus pulled up on their left side, and Djimmi and Mr. Chimes pulled up on their right. They batted the little car between them like a ping-pong ball.

"Hang on," Ms. Chalice said.

She steered to the left and bumped Brineybeard. Then she spun the wheel to the right and bashed Djimmi. The three little cars bumped and bashed and batted and banged one another mercilessly as they raced down the road.

Brineybeard pulled in close.

"Drop your anchor, you landlubbers!" he shouted, and reached for Cuphead.

From the other side, Mr. Chimes came at Ms. Chalice with his terrible cymbals.

"Eek, eek, eek!"

While Ms. Chalice held the wheel, Cuphead moved from side to side, fighting back the intruders. This went on for a considerable distance, and then something happened that brought the greatest bumper car race in the history of the Inkwell Isles to a swift and sudden end.

"Oh no," said Ms. Chalice.

It was an "oh no" moment if ever there was one. Up ahead, blocking the road, was a large carnival wagon. Standing in front of it was the whole gang—Beppi, Sally Stageplay, Cala Maria, Phear Lap, Pirouletta, the Yak-robats, the knife thrower, the human cannonball, the strongman, Cagney Carnation, the unicycling bear, the three turtles, Ernestine Elephant, and the derby-wearing duck.

Considering they'd only been at the carnival for a couple of hours, they'd made an impressive number of enemies.

"What'll we do now?" Ms. Chalice asked.

But Cuphead was out of ideas. They'd literally come to the end of the road. He was about to tell Ms. Chalice the bad news when he felt something on his shoulder. This wasn't surprising; his conscience always showed up at times like these. Only when he looked, he didn't see a little winged Cuphead.

He saw a little tin monkey.

In fact, he saw a lot of little tin monkeys.

Linked hand to hand, and tail to tail, the monkeys formed a chain that led all the way to the sky. Cuphead and Ms. Chalice looked up.

"Mugman!" they cheered.

There was Mugman, flying high overhead in one of the little airplanes from the kiddie ride.

"Climb aboard!" he said.

Cuphead and Ms. Chalice quickly shimmied up the chain of little monkeys and plopped into the airplane alongside Mugman. The angry crowd below shouted and hollered and used the kind of language you don't expect from carnival people, but it didn't matter. Mugman just grinned and waved, and steered into the nearest cloud.

Everything was going to be all right.

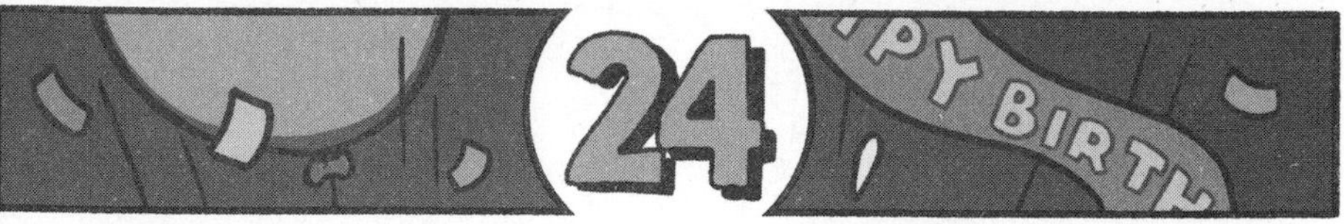

24

THE GREAT ESCAPE

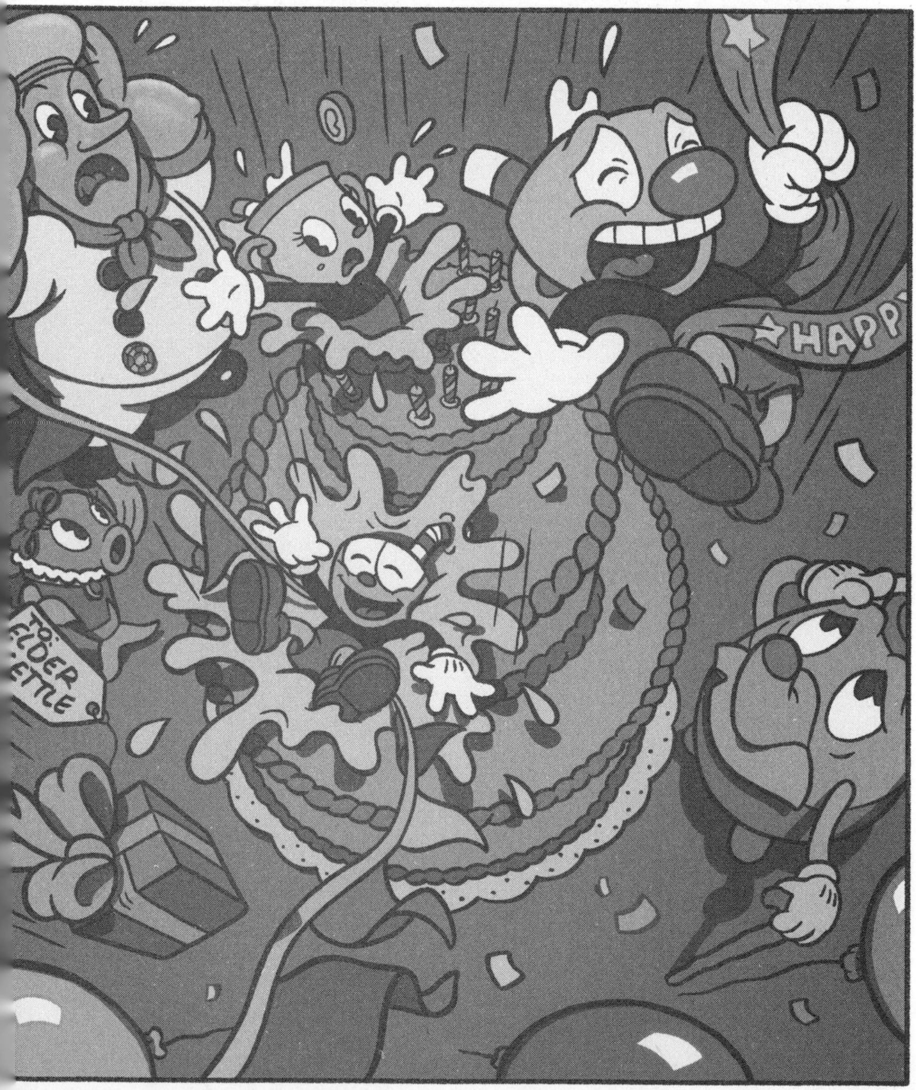
HAPPY

Or was it? You see, while most clouds were friendly, peaceful places open to everyone, Mugman had managed to find the one cloud that wasn't.

It was Hilda Berg's cloud.

Hilda hadn't forgotten what Cuphead's ball had done to her garden, or how those roughhousing daydreams had floated up and ruined the neighborhood. And as it happened, she'd just spotted the troublemakers behind it all right here in her own backyard. Obviously, they hadn't learned their lesson, but she'd fix that.

And it would be a lesson they'd never forget.

Cuphead was sitting back and enjoying the view (not that there was much view to enjoy—they were inside a cloud, you know) when he had the oddest feeling they were being watched. It was ridiculous, of course. Who'd be watching them up here?

He'd just put it out of his mind when, out of the

corner of his eye, he caught a glimmer of something. At first he couldn't make out what it was, but as it came closer, he realized . . . no, it couldn't be . . . it just couldn't be. . . .

But it was.

"Remember the airigolds!" Hilda shrieked.

Without warning, the angry zeppelin swooped in and fired.

Rat-a-tat-a-tat-a-tat!

Sploot! Sploot! Splat!

A squishy spray of tomatoes hit the tiny plane.

"She's got a salad shooter," Ms. Chalice yelled. "Look out!"

Mugman swerved. A second later, a cucumber missile came streaking through the air and Cuphead had to duck to avoid being vege-nated.

"That was too close. Let's get out of here!" Cuphead shouted.

Mugman wanted to oblige. Unfortunately, there was a problem with the wings—they were on fire. (It seems they'd been hit by some spicy jalapeño peppers, and if you've ever had one, you know how dangerous they are.) Still, they'd be all right as long as she didn't use a—

"Cantaloupe!" Cuphead yelled.

Mugman banked to the right, but it was too late. The melon clipped the plane's tail, sending it into a spin. By the time he pulled out of it, Hilda was on top of them. She flew in so close they could count the hairs in her spit curls.

"I told you what would happen if you ever crossed me again," she said. "And now I'll show you what a zeppelin can really do!"

They watched as Hilda pumped herself up bigger and bigger and bigger and bigger and—

"If there's one thing I can't stand, it's a blowhard," said Ms. Chalice, and she poked Hilda with a needle.

"*YOWWWWW!*" Hilda screamed.

There was a sudden loud hissing noise, and Hilda began zipping through the air like a deflating balloon.

"I'll get you for this!" she yelled. "I'll get all of *youuuuuuuuuu!*"

Same ol' Hilda. Cuphead and Ms. Chalice couldn't help laughing. But apparently Mugman could help it, because he wasn't laughing at all. He was listening.

Sput-sput-sputter...

"What's that sound?" Ms. Chalice asked.

"The plane," he told her. "We're going down."

It turned out Hilda's veggie assault had done more damage than they'd realized (if you know anything about kiddie-ride planes, you know they can handle only so much nutrition), which meant there was nothing left to do but—

"Jump!" Mugman said.

An instant later, Mugman, Ms. Chalice, and Cuphead had bailed out of the tiny plane and were falling helplessly through space.

"Any ideas?" Cuphead asked.

"We could make parachutes out of our underpants," said Mugman.

Cuphead shook his head. Then he looked over to Ms. Chalice.

"Flap our arms like birds?" she said.

And that's what they did. It didn't stop their plunging, but it was good exercise and it helped to pass the time.

Well, as you can see, the three friends were in quite a predicament. That's what happens when you're flying around with your head in the clouds. You lose sight of the big picture. And in this case, the big picture was what was happening at that very moment down on the ground.

You see, directly beneath them, a huge crowd had gathered in Pumpernickel Park for one of the largest birthday celebrations the Inkwell Isles had ever seen. Elder Kettle was there, grinning from ear to ear even though he was a little concerned that the children hadn't shown up yet. It wasn't like them. Oh well, he was sure they'd drop in any minute now. The important thing was that everyone had remembered his birthday—even Chef Saltbaker, who had just arrived with the cake.

And what a cake it was! Twelve layers high, each of them beautifully decorated with white candy flowers and sweet, creamy frosting. It was the fluffiest, sweetest, most beautiful cake the Inkwell Isles had ever seen. The candles up top turned it into a showpiece, and Chef Saltbaker smiled as he wheeled it toward the guest of honor.

"My dear friend Elder Kettle," Chef said. "I have created something very special just for you. May I present—"

SPLAT!

SPLAT!

SPLAAAAAAAAAAAAT!

Chef Saltbaker's magnificent creation splattered

like a freshly exploded watermelon. It wasn't supposed to, of course, but that's what happens when three late-arriving guests fall out of the sky and use it for a landing pad. All the guests were covered in sweet, creamy frosting (which they swore was the most delicious thing they'd ever worn), and the trees were painted with decorative candy flowers. A huge gasp rose up from the crowd as the sticky, gooey skydivers crawled out of the bottom layer. For a moment, there was an uneasy silence—then Mugman smiled. He had birthday candles where his teeth should be. Cuphead laughed. Ms. Chalice laughed. Everyone laughed.

Well, almost everyone.

"My cake! My beautiful cake!" Chef Saltbaker cried. "What have you done to my cake?"

As for Elder Kettle, he tried to look angry, but he just couldn't do it. He was too happy the three of them were all right, and that they'd made such a memorable entrance. Cuphead grinned and handed him a beautifully wrapped box. It immediately burst open, and out popped the Four Mel Arrangement.

It's your birthday, Elder Kettle, and we've come here to say
We're all glad to be with you on this very special day

And now it's time for something that should give you quite
  a lift
From all your friends and neighbors please enjoy this special
  gift!

The Mels handed him the gold watch and chain, and when he put it on, it looked even more stately and distinguished than Cuphead had imagined. Everyone agreed it was the nicest watch they'd ever seen, and they congratulated Cuphead, Mugman, and Ms. Chalice for finding the perfect present for Elder Kettle.

"Thank you all so much. It's been a grand birthday," Elder Kettle said.

And so Cuphead's story had a happy ending—at least it would have if it had ended right there. But, of course, it didn't. There was a little bit more to tell.

25

DOUBLE TROUBLE

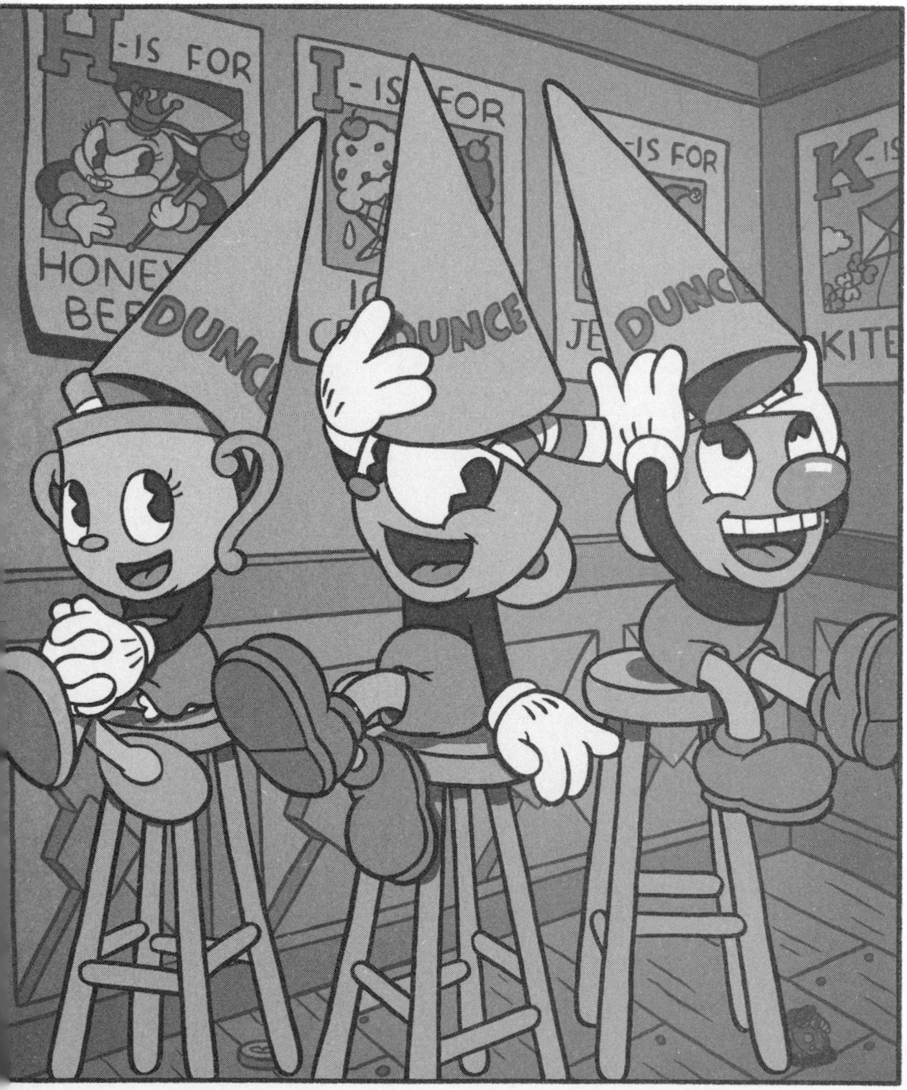

H-IS FOR
HONEY
BE
I-IS FOR
DUNCE
DUNCE
-IS FOR
DUNCE
K-IS
KITE

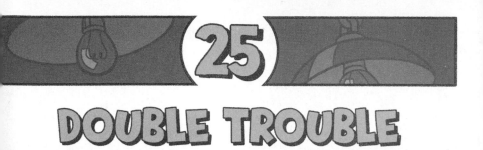

Cuphead walked into the classroom with Mugman and Ms. Chalice and put his books beside his desk, but he did not sit down. How could he? His desk was already occupied—by him.

"Cuphead?" Professor Lucien said.

There was an awkward silence.

"Someone seems to be sitting in your desk, Cuphead."

"So it would seem," said Cuphead.

"Curious thing, wouldn't you say?"

"Oh, absolutely," Cuphead agreed.

"And what's even more curious," the teacher continued, "is that Mugman and Ms. Chalice also have someone in their desks. Isn't that odd?"

"Very odd," said Cuphead.

"Spooky," said Ms. Chalice.

"It's a stumper, all right," said Mugman.

The professor strolled down the row of desks. He wasn't going to make this easy.

"Now, can any of you give me an explanation as to how this happened?"

"Doppelgänger?" said Cuphead.

"Evil twin?" said Ms. Chalice.

"Poorly devised escape plan that one of us deeply regrets?" said Mugman.

Cuphead and Ms. Chalice gave him a look.

"Very good, Mugman," Lucien said. "I think you're onto something."

The three of them stared at the floor. Even though they had a good reason for doing what they did, it was a pretty dirty trick.

"We're sorry, Professor. We shouldn't have done it. But can I ask a question?" Cuphead said. "Why are they wearing dunce hats?"

It was true. The fake versions of Cuphead, Ms. Chalice, and Mugman were all wearing long, cone-shaped hats with the word *DUNCE* written on the side.

Lucien smiled.

"Oh, those," he said. "They earned those by not knowing a single answer to the pop quiz."

"Pop quiz?" said Cuphead.

"They insisted I give them one," Lucien explained.

Cuphead, Mugman, and Ms. Chalice turned and stared at Mac. Mac gulped.

"I may have gotten carried away," he said.

At that moment, the door to the classroom opened and in walked Principal Silverworth.

"Ah, you're just in time," Lucien told him. "We were just discussing what to do about our sudden outbreak of look-alikes."

Silverworth wiped his monocle, stepped forward, and raised a finger in the air.

"Well, ordinarily I'd say a situation like this calls for one week's detention. But since we're seeing double..."

"Two weeks detention it is," Professor Lucien said.

The three friends looked at one another. Their mouths fell open.

"Did you just say two weeks?!" Cuphead moaned. "Gee whiz, Professor, I'm—"

He looked at the professor. He looked at Principal Silverworth. He looked at the dummy in his chair. It really was a ridiculous-looking thing. Cuphead pulled the hat from its head and put it on his own.

"I'm a dunce," he said, and then he laughed.

The next two weeks would be hard, but Cuphead couldn't complain. Elder Kettle had a great birthday, and that's all that mattered. And if he had to have detention, he couldn't ask for two better friends to have it with. He, Ms. Chalice, and Mugman would get through it together; he was sure of that.

Because together, they could get through anything.

THE END? NOPE!

Now that you've survived the chaos at the carnival, go back for another look at the images and see if you can find these hidden objects, characters, and bosses. Good luck!

Hidden Objects

COIN X 25

DICE X 5

CHARMS X 4

WEAPONS X 4

MUSHROOM X 4

LADYBUG X 4

BABY DRAGON X 3

BALLOON X 3

POKER CHIP X 3

ROCKET CLOWN X 3

FLYING FISH X 3

Hidden Characters

CANTEEN HUGHES X 1

TULLY X 1

BUSTER X 1

QUADRATUS X 1

CORA X 1

ANGEL X 1

GINGER X 1

Hidden Bosses

DEVIL X 1

DR. KAHL X 1

RIBBY & CROAKS X 1

BLIND SPECTER X 1

RUMOR HONEYBOTTOMS X 1

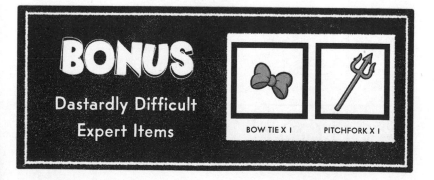

BONUS

Dastardly Difficult Expert Items

BOW TIE X 1

PITCHFORK X 1

ACKNOWLEDGMENTS

Once upon a time (which is when all the best stories begin), my mom and a couple of friends of hers started a tearoom. It was a pretty little place decorated with the kinds of things you'd expect to find in a Victorian parlor, but what I remember most are the teapots. I defy you to look at a teapot and not feel the need to speak to it. They have big, round faces and long, spoutlike noses and personalities all their own. And whenever I'd see one sitting on a table surrounded by cups and saucers and plates, I'd have the distinct impression I was watching a family out for a picnic. I'd completely forgotten about those days and probably would've never given them another thought—then I met Elder Kettle and Mugman and Cuphead.

I haven't looked at a table setting the same way since.

I'm profoundly grateful to Chad and Jared Moldenhauser for bringing Cuphead to life, along with all the other inhabitants of the amazing, magical Inkwell Isles (a clever little homage to another team of visionary brothers: founders of the legendary Out of the Inkwell, Inc.,) Max and Dave Fleischer. Working on this book was like leaping into a television screen and strolling through the great cartoons of history. So I owe an enormous debt to the Fleischers, Tex Avery, Walt Disney, Walter Lantz, and a slew of other early animators. Without them, dishes wouldn't dance, anvils wouldn't fall, and the world would be a lot less fun.

Speaking of fun, I had way too much of it on this project, and I'm completely okay with that. After all, if you can't have fun working with Brandi Bowles, Rachel Poloski, Samantha Schutz, Eli Cymet, Tyler Moldenhouer, and the phenomenal artists at Studio MDHR, then you're incapable of enjoying yourself and probably need to get a dog. As for how I got mixed in with this ridiculously talented group of people, all I can say is that sometimes the universe smiles at you for no good reason at all, and it's best not to ask any questions. The truth is, I'd have been lost without their guidance, patience, and spontaneous bursts of brilliance, and I can't thank them enough.

I also want to thank those friends and family members who served as guinea pigs while I experimented with various ideas for these pages. They listened longer than they needed to, laughed in all the right places, and pushed me through the word jungle and out the other side. Oh, and a special thanks to my nephew, Noah, who showed me what a spectacular experience the Cuphead video game is when it's played by someone with actual skills. I especially appreciated his advice (*"Stop dying."*) and have taken it to heart. A rematch awaits.

Finally, a tip of the hat to Boody Rogers, who told me stories years ago about working as a cartoonist in New York in the 1930s. They were always exciting and always funny and occasionally true, or at least true enough to make me wish I'd been born a few decades sooner.

Ron Bates is a novelist who writes about secret laboratories, bullies, evil robots, toilet monsters, super plumbers, cafeteria tacos, and all the other things that make being a middle-school student so interesting. A former newspaper reporter and humor columnist, he is the author of *How to Make Friends and Monsters*, *How to Survive Middle School and Monster Bots*, and *The Unflushables*. He also writes comic books, poems, and other stuff for kids who like to laugh. He lives in Texas.